Nina Allan lives in North Devon and is a previous winner of the British Science Fiction Award in 2014 with her novella *Spin*. In the same year, her second novella *The Gateway* was shortlisted for the Shirley Jackson Award. Her debut novel *The Race* was shortlisted for the Kitschies Red Tentacle, the British Science Fiction Award and the John W Campbell Memorial Award in 2015.

By the same author

A Thread of Truth
Microcosmos
The Silver Wind
Stardust
The Race

THE HARLEQUIN

Nina Allan

First published in Great Britain
and the United States of America in 2015
Sandstone Press Ltd
7 Dochcarty Road
Dingwall
Ross-shire
IV15 9UG
Scotland.

www.sandstonepress.com

The publisher acknowledges support from Creative Scotland
towards publication of this volume.

ISBN: 978-1-910124-38-3
ISBNe: 978-1-910124-39-0

Cover design by Jason Anscombe at Raw Shock
Typesetting by Iolaire Typesetting, Newtonmore
Printed and bound by Totem, Poland

For Maureen Weller

Beaumont's train came in just after midday. There was still snow on the ground, frozen to a treacherous shine and filthy with footprints. Outside Victoria station a line of cabs stood waiting at the kerb. As Beaumont picked his way along the icy pavement, he noticed Richard Ferguson emerging from the station buffet. At least he thought it was Ferguson. Beaumont moved back into the shadow of the station exit but it was too late, he had been spotted. Ferguson raised his hand and waved. He was wearing a long grey overcoat with horn buttons. It sat oddly on him, Beaumont thought, as if he'd gone off with another man's coat by mistake. There was stubble on Ferguson's cheeks, a shabby two-day growth that drew attention to rather than hid the broken line of reddened scar tissue that ran down from the corner of Ferguson's mouth into his shirt collar.

"Beaumont? It is Beaumont, isn't it? It's Dickie Ferguson."

Ferguson had arrived at Westcombe Priory as a new teacher the same year that Beaumont was due to take the Oxford entrance examination. On the few occasions they found reason to speak, Beaumont had addressed the man as Sir, or Mr Ferguson. The idea that he was now supposed to call him Dickie seemed preposterous and somehow distasteful. Beaumont felt no desire to renew the acquaintance, in any case. He couldn't see the point.

"It's good to see you," Beaumont said. "It's been a while."

"I heard you were –." Ferguson hesitated, no doubt thinking better of his eagerness to divulge exactly what it was he had heard. He glanced at Beaumont's army greatcoat, the battered brown leather valise. "You've been demobbed then, I see?"

"Six months ago," Beaumont said. "I've been in Paris."

"Paperwork?" said Ferguson.

"Something like that." Beaumont shrugged. He watched helplessly as the cab he had been about to get into was bagged by a woman whose broad hips were shrouded in what looked like a blue chenille dressing gown. Greasy-looking, brass-coloured curls straggled across her shoulders in an unkempt mass.

"Wicklow Street," she said. Her voice was strident, almost commanding, all South London vowels. Beaumont imagined what her body must be like beneath the hideous coat, the flesh still supple but not quite clean, wrapped about in the scents of dried-on sweat and boiled potato peelings. Beaumont's groin twitched. God knew what acts she had been driven to, just to get by.

"Would you care for a drink?" Ferguson was saying. "I'm buying."

It was the last thing Beaumont wanted, but he found himself saying yes, all the same, if only to put off the moment when he had to face Lucy.

"I don't have long," he said.

"A quick one, then. There's a place just round the corner."

Ferguson led the way. Beaumont noticed the way he

walked, in a ragged half-stride, no doubt the result of the same piece of ordnance that had messed up his face.

The pub, the King James, was packed. There was a large open fire in the saloon bar. A dog lay on the tiles in front of it, a lurcher or perhaps a borzoi, coffee-coloured with splotches of white. It raised its head in response to the draught from the open door. Its eyes, reflecting the firelight, gleamed gold as sovereigns. Beaumont had heard stories of men shooting dogs in the trenches, for extra food, though he'd never seen it happen himself. An omnibus thundered past outside, making the windows rattle. A shudder passed through Beaumont, the quickened heartbeat of unwelcome memories.

"We can sit here," Ferguson said. He made a gesture towards two free seats at a table on the right, close to the window. Cigarette smoke drifted, hauled in towards the centre of the room by the heat of the fire. As he made his way towards the window alcove, Beaumont felt himself jostled. He turned to see a swarthy man with an eye patch, his bristling, scoop-like hands clutching two bowls of what looked like Irish stew.

"Get your arse out of my face, nancy boy," said the man with the eye patch. "Sodding burnt myself now, haven't I?"

To Beaumont the man seemed degenerate, a throwback, almost Neanderthal. "I'm sorry," he said. He could smell the man's breath, the reek of warm beer and onions. Beaumont imagined letting fly at him, the brute thud of his closed fist in the man's podgy stomach, the twin bowls spilling their steaming contents over his face and chest. Like shit from the latrine, Beaumont thought.

"Just watch where you're going." The Neanderthal

eased himself into his seat. His companion dragged one of the bowls across the table and began to eat, blowing noisily on each spoonful of stew before slurping it into his mouth. The stew smelled of rancid fat and floury potatoes. Like pigswill. Beaumont thought of Paris, the corner café near the Pigalle metro station where each morning he had savoured a café au lait and practised his halting French on the waitress, whose name was Irène and who had given him an old bank account ledger to write in. Paper was scarce and Beaumont was grateful, but when he tried to kiss her she had turned roughly aside. Irène's impassive, porcelain features reminded him of a doll his sister Doris had once owned, Miss Misty, her head like a smooth round ball, her hair black lacquer. Irène's body though had been soft-looking and running to fat, like a much older woman's. Beaumont thought again of the woman he'd seen outside Victoria station, her greasy, brassy hair, the horrible blue coat that looked like a dressing gown.

He wondered if he would ever see Paris again.

"What'll you have?" Ferguson said.

"A pint of bitter, if that's all right."

"You look like you need it, if you don't mind my saying. Won't be a tick." He seemed delighted to see Beaumont unbend, even a little. Beaumont's mouth filled with saliva as he anticipated the taste of the beer, sour-strong and rank as herbs, the yellow aroma of smog and of the whole of London. He felt suddenly overcome, remembering the times – in the dugout, in the foul bedroom in Dieppe, in the ambulance with Stephen Lovell, for God's sake – when he thought he would never see Doris again, or Victoria station, or the house in Lambeth. He had never thought of Lucy at such times.

"Get this down you," Ferguson said. He set the beers on the table. Beaumont raised his glass and took a swallow, lowering his head to meet it halfway. His nostrils widened. The bitter coated his tongue and the roof of his mouth like a solution of peat and black treacle.

"That's good," he said. He found he was staring at Ferguson's face, the knotted train of scars, the untidy stubble. Beaumont supposed Ferguson had made a hero of himself. His type – considerate, upright, comradely, lovers of team sports – usually did. He felt a jarring contempt for Ferguson, the same sinking despair he'd felt when he first came upon Lovell, lying on his side in a wheel rut, trying to hold himself together with his filthy hands.

Ferguson seemed to have kept himself more or less in one piece, yet Beaumont could not escape the conviction that he was equally doomed.

Ferguson shifted in his seat, then raised a hand to his sewn-together cheek.

"It's nothing," he said. "Caught a bit of shrapnel, that's all."

"Where were you?"

"Somewhere in Belgium. I lost three toes off my right foot as well, but I was lucky. The chap next to me took it in the head." Ferguson gulped at his beer then turned to gaze into the fire. Beaumont cursed himself inwardly. He detested these conversations: the statistics, the place names, the running tally of mutilations and losses, yet here he was, less than half an hour back in London and already caught up in one. And with Ferguson too, a man he barely knew and hoped never to see again after today.

Ferguson coughed and took out his smokes. He offered the pack to Beaumont, who shook his head. Ferguson placed a cigarette between his own lips and lit it, not with the flip-over army lighter Beaumont expected but with a match from a packet of Swan Vestas he had retrieved from the pocket of his overcoat. His lips were full and rosy, like a woman's, almost exactly matching the colour of the scar on his face.

"Do you have any plans?" he said. He drew deeply and, Beaumont thought, gratefully on the cigarette. He sensed that Ferguson was only asking this question out of politeness, the same artfully ingrained Englishness that prevented him from asking what he really wanted to know, which was where had Beaumont served and what had he done. He had no doubt that someone – one of the other masters, probably – would have told Ferguson about the hearing, about the fight outside the pub with the thugs who had called him a coward and threatened to cut off his balls.

The only question Ferguson wanted to ask was whether Beaumont had seen anything of the war, or if he had spent it behind a desk, filling in forms.

"I drove ambulances," Beaumont said. "And supply trucks. I dug latrines. Anything that didn't involve putting bullets into actual people. And no, I have no plans. Not yet." He felt surprised at the strength of his anger, which he had thought he was through with. Beaumont had seen men die, but he had not killed a man. He had been shot at, but refrained from shooting back. In the eyes of the thugs outside the Lambton Arms, his application to the tribunal made him a coward. In the eyes of his sister Doris, they made him a hero. He did not know what they made him in the eyes of his fiancée, Lucy.

In the eyes of Richard Ferguson he read only relief.

"You must have been in a few tight corners," Ferguson said. He seemed to relax slightly, and Beaumont sensed he had passed some kind of test. He found himself having to repress the urge to laugh out loud.

"Some," he said. He took another long swig of his beer. He realised he was hungry. He watched the man with the eye patch and his piggy companion wolfing their stew. He tried to imagine what it might feel like to be inside the Neanderthal's head, to think his thoughts. He experienced a brief, slurping sensation of warmth and mild disgruntlement and food. He looked over towards the bar, where a woman was serving drinks and another, younger woman, her daughter probably, was cleaning glasses. The younger woman glanced across at him and smiled. She was hopelessly ugly, her features scarred with pockmarks, a permanent reminder, no doubt, of some disease or other indignity suffered in childhood. Unlike the pig man and his friend she exuded strength. Belatedly, Beaumont smiled back, but the woman had already turned away and did not notice. A short while later she disappeared through a door behind the bar.

Beaumont realised with a start that he and Ferguson were the youngest men there.

"I should go," he said to Ferguson. There was a sudden draught of cold air as the street door opened. A man entered, short and stocky, his shoes encased in rinds of melting snow. Beaumont watched as he approached the bar, hands thrust deep into the pockets of his overcoat which, now that Beaumont came to look at it, seemed not to be one garment so much as several. The main body of the coat was grey, an army greatcoat not unlike Beaumont's but even older. The left sleeve appeared to have been taken from one of the stiff black stuff overcoats most commonly worn by coal hauliers or the rag-and-bone men who worked the teeming, disease-ridden streets of Hackney and Islington. The right sleeve was from a sheepskin jacket. The strip of mangy woollen fleece at the wrist was stained a putrid yellow.

When the man turned to look at him, Beaumont saw that one of his eyebrows had been burned away. The scab that replaced it had the blackish-brown lustre of burnt sugar.

Beaumont felt an unnatural stillness come over him. Although the noise of the pub was now close to deafening, he was somehow still able to hear the ragged, stilted susurrus of his own breathing. For a moment he was back in the ambulance, smelling the overpowering stink of shit, hearing the soft, grunting moans of Stephen Lovell, curled tight as a clenched fist around his spilled intestines. He saw the face at the window, the hand, hammering to be let in, the palm criss-crossed with cuts from barbed wire, the dark semicircle of nameless grime under the nails.

I know the way. You have to trust me, or this man will die. The man at the window had called himself Vladek. Beaumont had never known if this was his first name or his surname. It seemed not to matter.

Lovell had died anyway, but later, on a sodden piece of churned up pastureland behind a burned-out farmhouse, the man with the torn hands told Beaumont the coat he wore had been sewn together from the remains of the garments of ten dead soldiers.

That's the thing about wartime, Vladek said. *Nothing goes to waste*.

Beaumont felt he would know his face anywhere.

Beaumont saw these things for a second, then the background din of the pub burst in on him again and the man at the bar was just a heavyset stranger in a coal stoker's coat with the stitching torn along the length of one of its sleeves. With or without the coat, he could have been anybody.

"Poor devil," said Ferguson quietly. "His face is gone."

It was only then that Beaumont realised it was not just the man's eyebrow that was missing. The whole left side of his face was missing also. His features had been reduced to raw flesh then twisted into a pink, corrugated mass of scar tissue.

Ferguson left his seat and approached the bar. For some reason Beaumont felt convinced that Ferguson meant to throw the faceless man out. He watched as Ferguson reached into his pocket, handing the man his cigarettes and what looked to Beaumont like a ten-shilling note. When the man reached to take it, Beaumont saw he was also missing two of his fingers. Off to one side the pig man and the Neanderthal with the eye patch had finished shovelling down their food and started to play cards.

I am still in hell, Beaumont thought. Only now it is worse, because everyone pretends that the life we are living is the life we want. The noise of the pub seemed overwhelming, stiff with the rising heat of unwashed bodies. Beaumont feared he might vomit. When Ferguson returned to their table, Beaumont told him he really should be going.

"You'll be wanting to get home, of course," Ferguson said. "It was selfish of me to keep you. Forgive me."

They left the King James together, and for an awful moment Beaumont thought Ferguson was going to insist on accompanying him back to Lambeth. Much to his relief, this did not happen. Ferguson excused himself, saying he had an appointment.

"It's a work thing I can't get out of," he said. From the look of him, unshaven and dishevelled, Beaumont doubted it. He wondered who Ferguson was really meeting, if in fact he was meeting anyone at all, or if, like Beaumont himself, he simply wanted to be alone.

"It's been good to see you," Ferguson said. "You must look me up once you're settled, and we can do this again." He clapped Beaumont hard on the shoulder, applying a gentle squeeze before removing his hand. Beaumont stiffened instinctively, remembering the things some of his schoolfellows had said, the younger ones who still took PT and who made jokes about what Dickie Ferguson got up to in the showers. Get your arse out of my face, nancy boy, Beaumont thought. He supposed he should feel repulsed, but instead he felt tired. He had seen eighteen-year-old artillerymen shot for less than what had just happened with Ferguson.

"Take care, Dickie," he said quietly. "Thanks for the drink." He turned away before Ferguson could answer and started walking, turning left on Wilton Road and then right onto Vauxhall Bridge Road. He headed south, noting the bricked-up doorways and whitewashed windows of businesses that had failed or closed their doors because of the war. Piles of filthy snow stood at the kerbside. In the litter-strewn alleyway beside a tobacconist's shop a child sat, huddled against a coal bunker, a dry-looking crust of bread between its grubby hands. Beaumont had seen similar sights in Paris, but the beauty of certain women, the burnt sienna scent of roasting coffee, the difficulty of understanding the language beyond the most basic level had insulated him from the harshness of everyday reality.

He thought of an amusement arcade he had once visited with Doris, on the West Pier in Brighton. He particularly remembered a display of automata, a series of intricately constructed domestic interiors sealed inside wooden cases behind a glass panel. When you put a farthing into the slot, the scene came to life. A woman in an empire-waist dress watered chrysanthemums, a gentleman in a silken waistcoat read the newspaper. Lights switched themselves on. A spotted terrier scooted across the polished parquet floor.

Could all of that be gone? Beaumont headed east along Millbank, then across the Lambeth Bridge to the southern embankment. He knew he could catch a bus on Lambeth Road that would bring him to Kennington Lane in under ten minutes, but he decided to walk instead. He crossed the Embankment Road and carried on along Black Prince Road until he reached the junction with Kennington Road. The rush hour was still some way off, and so traffic was light. As he crossed into Kennington Lane he saw a woman in a fox fur coat stepping out of a hackney carriage. Her outline shimmered like a mirage against the gridiron of naked trees. The snow on the streets here was still white, white as royal icing or hospital sheets, and Beaumont began to walk more slowly, looking closely about him. He was almost home.

Since the death of Stephen Lovell, the house on Kennington Lane had begun to seem unreal to him. He had been born in that house, lived there his whole life until the war came. The Kennington house had always been a constant, the most permanent aspect of his life, yet being apart from it and in such circumstances had lent it the aspect of a mirage. In the ambulance with Lovell, he found himself increasingly unwilling to believe he would ever return there. Afterwards, in Paris, he had sometimes found himself unable even to picture the house or Kennington Lane itself. In his mind the stoutly angled edifice of London stock had always been synonymous with stability, with durability, impervious to change. The war had taught him that nothing was impervious to change, that the most durable-seeming reality could be reduced to horror and chaos in less than a second.

The house on Kennington Lane had begun to take on more and more the aspect of something imagined, a place glimpsed once in a dream and then lost forever. He remembered his friend Ambrose Weston telling him about a new novel that had just been published in France, a fantasy called *Le Grand Meaulnes* by a poet and literary critic named Alain-Fournier.

"*Meaulnes* is not a fantasy," Ambrose insisted. "Memory is not fantasy. It is the bridge between the real and the imagined."

They were at the training camp at North Allerton. Beaumont's instinct was to reject the novel, which from what Ambrose was saying seemed mainly to be about a young man's obsessive quest for the perfect woman. He was able to turn down his friend's offer to lend him the book on the grounds that his French was nowhere near good enough, but in the weeks and months following the Armistice he found his thoughts returning to it constantly. He eventually discovered a copy in a murky, cigar-smoked bookshop in Montmartre and had purchased it at once, even though his funds were desperately low and his command of French, though improved, still made a fluent reading impossible.

In the evenings in his room near Pigalle he had spent hours poring over the text by the light of the foul-smelling kerosene lamp that provided the only illumination he could afford. He was still some way from finishing the novel, but the early passages, where Meaulnes first comes to the school, released in Beaumont a sense of keen regret that he came to associate increasingly with the house on Kennington Lane. He longed to discuss his feelings with Ambrose Weston but that was now impossible. Ambrose had gone missing in action some six months before the Armistice.

Ambrose Weston's father was an Anglican minister, and Ambrose himself had been intending to be ordained. As a man of the cloth, Ambrose could have claimed exemption from military service, but his brand of religion – fierce, intellectually demanding and unsparing of self – had driven him to see this as impossible. Implausibly, he had enjoyed military life. He liked the order, the comradeship. Now he was gone. There was a hole in Beaumont's mind where Ambrose Weston used to exist, unreachable and unreal as Meaulnes's Lost Domain.

The house was still there. In the part of his mind that remained from before, he knew it was insane of him to have doubted that it would be, yet he found himself staring at it with surprise, even with fear. The paintwork was in need of attention, and there was a noticeable build-up of grime on the downstairs window panes. Otherwise, the house was as it always had been, its four storeys seemingly inviolate behind their neatly aligned defence of cast iron railings.

Beaumont stood immobile for a moment, shifting his shabby valise from one hand to the other. Then he walked up the short front pathway and pulled the bell. He heard a woman's voice call out, a faint response from somewhere deeper inside the building, then footsteps hurrying lightly along the hall. He tried to remember how Lucy's footsteps sounded but was unable to. It was more than a month since he had written to Lucy. Since his demob she had sent him a letter every couple of days, care of the *poste restante* at Pigalle, asking ever more insistently when he would be returning. He kept his answers as vague as he could without actually lying, but in the end, sickened by his own mendacity, he'd stopped writing to her altogether.

Beaumont had just enough time to wonder if he should perhaps have telegraphed ahead to announce his arrival before the door was flung open and his sister was in his arms.

"Dennis," she said. "It is you! Oh, thank God."

He held her close, feeling her palms pressing against the back of his greatcoat and thinking how strange it felt to hear his Christian name. The war had remade him as Beaumont, except to the prostitutes he visited occasionally in Pigalle, who had spoken his name in the French way: *Denis*. He kissed the top of Doris's head. The tidily cropped, dunnock-brown hair was streaked with grey, and he felt another jolt of unreality pass through him as he wondered if he, like Meaulnes, had been spirited away for half a lifetime instead of just three years.

"Sorry to turn up out of the blue like this," he said. "I wasn't sure how long it might take me to get here. The trains are still all over the place." He paused. "Is Lucy here?"

"Lucy's out. She'll be back in an hour. Come on, this is ridiculous, talking out here on the step like this. Get yourself inside."

Doris stood to one side to let him pass, and Beaumont felt himself relax a little, knowing he would not have to face Lucy immediately, that he had time to compose himself, to decide what to say. He was relieved to see that, aside from the grey in her hair, Doris looked unchanged. Now that the first shock of their reunion was past, her face had returned to its habitual expression of calm preparedness. Doris was nicely made. She had never been beautiful but she had always been pleasant to look at, not least because of the clear intelligence that animated her, even when she was silent, which was often. Beaumont could not remember ever having seen her demonstrably angry on any subject except politics.

In so many ways she was the opposite of Lucy. Beaumont didn't suppose Lucy cared much if women won the vote or not. On the other hand, she was often angry. Dennis sometimes thought it was Lucy's anger he had fallen in love with, her insistence on expressing herself in such forthright terms.

He wondered what Lucy thought of the war. It came to him that in his letters he had barely mentioned it, though he had often found himself trying to imagine how she might have managed if the war had reached out and touched her directly. It was not the possibility of his own death he was thinking about – he thought he knew better than she how shallowly this would have affected her, at least in the long term – but how she would have coped with living alone, like Irène the waitress at the Café Paradis, with being on her feet until late in the evening, constantly acceding to the demands of others, perhaps in ways she could scarcely bear even to name.

Would such a life have destroyed her, or turned her into another person, stronger and more resourceful than the Lucy he had proposed to in a fit of ardour he regretted more or less as soon as it dawned on him there was no going back on it? For the briefest of moments, Beaumont imagined her on her knees in a hotel bedroom while the man with the burned away face fumbled with her underclothes. Beaumont had not been to bed with Lucy. There had been a time when he had tormented himself with his desire for her, so acute it sometimes felt like a physical illness. More recently though it had been Irène he fantasised about, her perfectly finished, doll-like head, its curious disjuncture with her peasant's body.

"Come through to the kitchen," Doris said. "I'll make us some tea."

Beaumont put down his suitcase. He looked at the floor, the calmly repeating pattern of black and white tiles, wondering if his room in the attic was still his, or whether it had been let out to paying guests, like his father's old room.

"Tea sounds perfect," he said. He hoped Doris could not smell the beer on him. Going to the pub with Ferguson had been a mistake, if only because the sight of the creature with the shattered face had reawakened memories he'd spent the past six months in Paris trying to forget.

"Are you all right, Den?" Doris said. "You look exhausted." She laid a hand on his arm, and for the first time Beaumont seemed properly to see his surroundings: the green-painted hall with its scrubbed tiles, the three engravings from Pevsners, hanging one above the other on the wall just inside the door. Clear daylight filtered through from the back, where the kitchen was, and the lean-to conservatory that ran off it, with its glass roof, its blue and white porcelain planters, Doris's carefully nurtured collection of cacti and succulents. Beyond that, the garden, with its russet walls. He saw it clearly in his mind's eye, the mown grass covered with snow, the rooks bunched in the criss-crossed branches of the empty trees.

"I'm fine," Beaumont said. "I haven't slept much this past day or so, that's all."

"You're bound to feel strange," said Doris. It was just like Doris to try and understand, to make excuses for him, Beaumont thought. The seeming futility of it cut deeply into him. He sat in the ancient beadwork chair that had been part of the kitchen's furnishings since he was a boy, while his sister ran water into the kettle and lit the gas. The chair stood in the corner, by the boiler, and Beaumont found himself doing automatically what he'd always done when he sat in it, leaning over to lace his fingers into the metal grid of the boiler guard, luxuriating in the familiar accumulation of heat, the faint smell of oil that had always given the kitchen something of the atmosphere of a machine shop.

Doris reached up to the dresser and took down the tea caddy, the same square tin they had always kept tea in, embossed with an enamelled Chinoiserie design of birds and peach blossom that seemed to embody everything he'd left behind here, the whole life-enhancing, God-granted expanse of it. He thought of his room upstairs, the chintz curtains and candlewick bedspread, the glass-fronted bookcase filled with texts by von Clausewitz and Machiavelli and Archimboldo, the tag ends, the abandoned remnants of his interrupted life.

I'll die here, he thought. He thought of his chilly little room in Paris with its single cold water tap and blackened floorboards, and longed for it with such intensity that it took the full force of his will to prevent himself from getting up from his chair, grabbing his valise from where it stood in the hallway and heading back to the station.

It was as if he could smell the approach of death, the foul-breathed monstrosity with poisoned meat under its nails he had narrowly escaped in Cassaron, its footfalls measured not in gunshots this time but in the languid, lustrous tick-tick-tick of the grandfather clock that stood in the niche alcove on the first floor landing. Beaumont asked himself which kind of death would be worse and could not answer. All he knew was that the old life could not be returned to. It was better to leave before he fell into it, inch by stupefied inch, and lost himself forever.

It would only take a second, and he would be free.

"Here you are," Doris said. "I've been saving this specially." She set the teapot on the table in front of him and poured his cup. The tea was fragrant and steaming. A lump of sugar gleamed in his saucer like a cube of quartz. The tea at the Front was bitter and grey. The older soldiers used to swear it was cut with iron filings. Beaumont had almost forgotten how real China tea tasted. He sipped the fragrant liquid, relishing its scent, its extraordinary power to soothe, and asked Doris how she had been managing.

"Things are easier with Dad gone. I know I shouldn't say that, but it's true." She sat very straight, with her cup in front of her, looking down. "The money I get from his room is useful too."

"I'm sorry," Beaumont said. He was not exactly certain what he was apologising for. Their father had died almost exactly four months after Armistice Day, of some monstrous, creeping disease that had never been named. Lucy had written to him about it, of how his father had been towards the end, in so much pain, finally, that the morphine the doctors prescribed could only bring him relief for a few short hours. Beaumont had dreaded those letters, not for the dreadful snapshots of suffering they contained – he had seen worse at the Front – but for the sense of guilt they aroused in him, the suspicion that Lucy and perhaps Doris also blamed him for not sharing their burden, for having, in one sense at least, evaded his duty.

But that was nonsense, of course. When Doris finally wrote to inform him of their father's death, she urged him to stay on in Paris, if that was what he wanted, that the worst was behind them.

"He asked for you," Doris said. "We told him you were in Paris, studying at the Sorbonne. He seemed pleased about that." She took a swallow of tea. "Listen, Den, you mustn't be angry with Lucy, she's had a hard time."

"I'm not angry with her."

"Yes, you are. I've sensed it for weeks now. At least give yourself time to get to know her again, properly. That's all I ask. Do you know what she's doing right now?"

"I have no idea."

"She's seeing about a lease for a place on Kennington Road. She's going to open a dress shop. She's been full of it for months."

"She didn't say anything about this in her letters."

"That's because she wanted it to be a surprise. A surprise for you. I'm telling you, Den, she's grown up a lot since you left. Give her a chance."

Beaumont fell silent. The idea of Lucy undertaking

anything that constituted independent action was so alien to his conception of her that he was unable to find a space for it in his mind. It was true that she had some money of her own, but they had not got around to discussing what they might do with it. Beaumont had vaguely supposed she would use it to help them set up home together. He had never imagined her with purpose, with plans.

The thought of a Lucy with plans made him feel tired. He could not bring himself to believe in her as a successful businesswoman – she grew bored too easily. The money and its part in their future would most likely be wasted.

"I think I'll go and unpack," he said to Doris.

"Just relax, Den. Try to, anyway. Let things happen to you for a bit. You'll soon start to feel better, you'll see."

She smiled, but she looked sad, and Beaumont could not escape the notion that he had, in some deep and irrevocable way, disappointed her. Contrition filled him, and he felt seized by the desire to hold his sister in his arms and tell her once again that he was sorry, to reassure her that all was well, that he needed some time to adjust but that he would soon be himself again.

Such simple words, and so much the right words that Beaumont could feel his eyes filling with tears at the thought of saying them. Perhaps, if he willed it hard enough, he could even make them true.

We all start out hungry for this world, Vladek had said. *But few of us find meat rich enough to satisfy that hunger.*

Beaumont had remembered the man's words when he first began reading *Le Grand Meaulnes*. He saw at once that Meaulnes was a being possessed by hunger, that it was his hunger that kept him vigorous and sane. The important thing was the hunger itself, not its satisfaction.

Before the war, Beaumont had dreamed of writing a treatise on the folly of empire that would stun the world. He wondered if the Front had turned him into the kind of man whose hunger might reasonably be satisfied by being the husband of a woman who ran a dress shop on the Kennington Road.

He sighed, and realised he really was exhausted.

"I'll be fine," he said. "I need a good night's sleep, that's all."

He swallowed the dregs of his tea and stood up, resting his hand briefly against the chair-back for support. Doris bent to retrieve his cup. Beaumont found himself wondering how much she knew of men, if she had perhaps had a love affair. He noticed again the flecks of grey in her hair.

"There's no need to come up," he said. "Let Lucy know I'm home when she gets in." He retrieved his case from the hall, then slowly climbed the stairs to his room. The house, in the main, seemed much as he remembered it. Beaumont's father had lectured in Pathology at the nearby King's College Hospital. Once he became too ill to go on working, Doris had taken the decision to rent out rooms, at first to medical students then, as more and more of the young men were called up, to anyone who could and would pay.

The Chinese rugs on the upper landings had been removed, presumably because Doris feared they would become ruined by the continual passage of feet up and down the stairs. The base linoleum was oiled and clean. From inside one of the rooms on the first floor, Beaumont could hear the dry tap-tap-tap of someone working at a typewriter, but otherwise the house was curiously silent.

Lucy's room, he knew, was on the first floor at the back, where his mother's sewing room used to be. It was a sunny room, south-facing, and he could understand why Lucy had commandeered it, though whether she knew it had been his mother's he had no idea.

He hesitated outside on the landing then pushed open the door. The room, as Beaumont had expected, was empty. The curtains stood half-closed, the thin strip of light between them gleaming with the blue-tinted radiance of sunlight on snow. A brown-and-black-checked day dress lay across the bed. On the night stand stood a Bristol Blue glass jug of dried flowers, beside it the framed photograph of himself that had been taken the day he went up to Oxford for his entrance interview.

The room was neat, uncluttered, and in some inexplicable way so much unlike the Lucy he remembered that Beaumont felt a sense of impropriety at being there. He glanced quickly around, then closed the door softly behind him and went on up the stairs. Lucy was the daughter of one of Beaumont senior's former colleagues, an esteemed surgeon who had undertaken work in Africa and in the Middle East. When the ship carrying him home from Aden was sunk, with all hands, by a German torpedo, Doris had insisted that Lucy come and live at Kennington Lane.

Beaumont had known Lucy since they were both sixteen. At that time, Beaumont had believed that the only real difference between them was that Lucy was used to having money. Now he was beginning to think he knew nothing about her.

There were three rooms in the attic: a washroom and closet, a box room, and the room that had been his own from the age of twelve. Beaumont was relieved to find that the box room had not been let out. He had quickly become used to close quarters in the army, but he would not have welcomed the presence of a stranger in an area he considered his personal domain. His bed was made up. He wondered how often Doris had been up to change the sheets since he'd been demobbed. He laid his suitcase on the bed then crossed to the casement window and looked out. The snow-decked roofs and gardens of Lambeth stretched away below him in their accustomed patterns. The view was so familiar, yet entirely strange, like a first, uncomprehending glimpse of a foreign city.

He stepped away from the window and opened his valise. There was not much inside: three clean shirts, his discharge papers, a pocket French dictionary and his dog-eared copy of Alain-Fournier's *Le Grand Meaulnes.* There was a photograph of Lucy, the leather-bound notebook he had used, when he was first drafted, to jot down the chapter headings for the thesis he still planned to write when he returned. Later, in Paris, the notebook became a repository for lists of French words he was trying to memorise, the names and addresses of army acquaintances he had promised to write to but never would.

Beside the notebook lay a silver napkin ring he had retrieved from the wreckage of the farmhouse where he had talked with Vladek, and listened to Stephen Lovell dying in the back of the ambulance. There was also Stephen Lovell's identity tag, a slim folder of papers that had also belonged to him and a silver locket that contained a curl of red-gold hair. Beaumont had read through the papers after Lovell died, but could make little sense of them. They seemed to be letters, or perhaps a diary, about the war, but they were not the kind of letters you could ever send home. The lock of hair belonged to Lovell's fiancée. Lovell had made Beaumont promise to go and see her once he was back in England.

"I can't promise," Beaumont said, even though Lovell was almost dead by then. What he meant was, it seemed wrong to make a promise when there was no guarantee he would survive long enough to fulfil it. He could be dead within the week, just like Lovell.

Lovell seemed to guess his thoughts. He grimaced through blood-flecked lips.

"You'll make it," he whispered. "Please."

In the end Beaumont had promised, not knowing whether he intended to keep his word or not. He had hidden Lovell's things away inside his suitcase, and through all the weeks and months in Paris he had not looked at them once. Seeing them again now, in the familiar and orderly context of his childhood room, gave him a feeling of disjuncture so severe it was almost as if he were hallucinating. Suddenly he knew he would do what Lovell had wanted. He would go to the girl and give her Lovell's things. There was not much he could do for Lovell, but at least this was something.

For a moment, he imagined Vladek grinning. He suppressed the image with an effort, thrust it away. Rose, he thought. The girl's name is Rose. He thought of how the garden was in summer, the ramble of yellow roses on the back wall, yellow as sulphur and blowsy pink, their entwined stems a mass of shiny green leaves and rust-coloured thorns.

He saw Vladek's hands, rent open in several places from the barbed wire. Vladek had staunched the flow of blood with mud from the ground. His trick had worked, though Beaumont had not liked to think about what might be mixed with the mud, how unclean it was. He had shut away thoughts of tetanus, Vladek's stocky frame bent over backwards in a half-circle of madness.

Oh stop, Beaumont thought. You know you're safe here. He looked down at the bed, the white sheets, the yellow candlewick bedspread. Far below him in the downstairs hallway he heard the sound of the front door being unlocked and opened, the tattoo of footsteps, the low murmur of women's voices. Suddenly, Beaumont could feel his heart hammering. He knew that in less than a minute Lucy would be here, upstairs, with him.

He realised he hadn't the slightest idea how he felt.

She entered the room without knocking, and Beaumont had just a few seconds to wonder how many times she had been up here during his absence. She was wearing a woollen dress, dark green and similar in style to the garment he'd seen lying on her bed downstairs. Her fair hair was drawn back from her face in a wide velvet band. Her cheeks were flushed, though whether this was from the cold of the outside air or the shock of seeing him again Beaumont could not tell.

"Den," Lucy said. "Oh, Den."

She crossed the room in three quick strides, wrapping her arms about his shoulders, laying her face against his chest. Beaumont felt he should hold her at least, but she was pinning his arms to his sides and so he could not.

She smelled of cold air, of snow. Beaumont remembered a snowball fight they'd had once, in the Bishop's Park, very soon after they met and when Beaumont first began to realise he might be falling in love with her.

Lucy had been wearing a black fur hat, a gift bought for her by her father during one of his regular sojourns in Eastern Europe. You look like you have a bear on your head, Beaumont had mocked her. A bear cub, at least. She had landed a direct hit on the side of his face then, a fist-sized, firmly packed snowball that hurt a great deal more than he had let on. She's magnificent, he thought. He had no experience of girls, not really, aside from Doris, but he had been filled with the overwhelming conviction that he did not want to be parted from Lucy, not ever, that their lives were destined to be interwoven from that moment on.

She was like a tall and well shaped flame that he wanted to guard.

Old crow's nest, Beaumont thought. That had been his nickname for her, in the old days, because she was so tall and because her fine curly hair tangled so easily in the wind and because her surname was Crosier.

He had never truly believed he would see her again.

Lucy raised her head and gazed into his face. Her eyes were the same greyish-green, the colour of serpentine.

"You're home," she said, and smiled. She let out a long sigh, and Beaumont felt her whole body tremble. "I know it's been forever, and I know things haven't been right, but before you say anything, I want you to know that everything is going to be better from now on."

"Lucy," Beaumont said. The sound of her name in his mouth took him aback, so weightless somehow, like two musical notes. It came to him that Lucy meant light.

"I don't want you to decide anything now," she went on quickly. "Let's wait awhile. You need time to settle." She laid her face again briefly against his chest. "Den, I've been so scared. I'm so happy to see you, to see you alive. The only thing that matters is that you're safe." She paused. "I heard about Ambrose. I've been aching to say something, but I couldn't write to you about it, it seemed too terrible to talk about in a letter. I know how much you love him." She hesitated. "I keep hoping for a miracle."

Beaumont felt stunned, almost stupefied. The things Lucy was saying to him were so different from what he had imagined. He had expected her to scold him, either implicitly or straight out, for not having answered her letters, the sharp little joke, the brittle laughter followed by the hardening of all her features as she revealed the core of her bitter feeling against him. Lucy was the same age as Beaumont, and an inch taller, but in his thoughts, he realised, she had always been younger, a child with a child's selfish concerns. The Lucy in front of him was someone different. He found he barely knew what to say to her.

He took her in his arms at last, staring over his shoulder at the black zipper that fastened her dress, dozens of shiny black teeth, locked together along the curving length of her spinal column.

"We can only hope," he said at last. "Missing doesn't mean dead, remember. Ambrose would want us to hope." He took a step backwards, keeping both hands on her shoulders. Rather than being disconcerting, as he knew it would be for some men, Lucy's height had always fascinated him. She gazed at him steadily. Beaumont realised with a shock that she looked older.

"I hear you're planning to go into business," he said. He found himself increasingly preoccupied with looking at her, fascinated by how well she seemed to fit the room, this house, the cleanliness and order of their surroundings. He thought how well made she was, the delicate angles of her shoulders and neck, the pale, silken curve of her hairline, her hair, sweeping upwards under the velvet band, bowing outwards very slightly above her high, white forehead. There was harmony in her being. The image of Irène, with her mismatched doll's head and peasant's body, seemed suddenly coarse and inappropriate beside her.

She is lovely, Beaumont thought. I had forgotten that. He saw a blush spreading up from beneath the neck of her dress, and her cheeks flushed a deeper shade of pink.

"Has Doris told you already? Oh, I wish she hadn't done that." She dropped her arms to her sides. "I wanted to tell you myself. To explain."

"Are you sure this is what you want? You never mentioned wanting to find a job before?" Beaumont regretted his choice of words almost immediately – he knew how quick Lucy could be to take offence – but Lucy seemed unperturbed.

"That's just it. This is all so new to me, and I know it will be hard for you to believe, at first anyway, but I am crazy for it. I've become a complete bore on the subject – ask Doris. She's been teaching me how to prepare proper business accounts and everything. I found the shop premises myself, through the classifieds. And it's all because of the war."

"The war?"

"I've hated feeling so helpless, Den. When Daddy died I went into a sort of cocoon of self-pity. But when your letters stopped coming I felt so afraid. I kept thinking that if you were killed it would all be my fault for not caring enough, about anything. For going through life so selfishly. I know how foolish that sounds, but it changed everything. I told myself it was up to me now, to make a difference. And with the shop I'll be able to make money for us. You can go back to Oxford and finish your studies. It's what I've dreamed of for months." She stopped speaking abruptly. "We weren't supposed to talk about this until later. I know it's too much, all at once."

"No," Beaumont said. He reached out and took her hand, her left hand, where the ring he had given her the evening before he left for North Allerton glinted softly on her fourth finger. It was a poor ring, a narrow band of gold set with three chip diamonds, but it was all he could afford. Now he thought how well it suited her, its simplicity a perfect match for the understated modesty of her dress. Her hand nestled palm to palm with his own, as if seeking shelter there. "I'm surprised, but that doesn't mean I don't like the idea. But I'm not expecting you to keep me, Lucy, I want you to know that. It wouldn't be right."

"Why on Earth not?" Her eyes flashed, and Beaumont caught a glimpse of the old Lucy, the Lucy who could throw herself into a passion if they happened to be late for a dinner engagement or if she burned a saucepan of toffee, only now her anger seemed less like a fit of pique and more like a deliberate determination to be heard. "Why should it always be the man? You want to study – it's what you've wanted for years. I want to open this shop. It all makes perfect sense. What does it matter who actually brings in the money when it's for both of us equally?"

Beaumont laughed. He couldn't help it. "What's happened to you, old crow's nest? You sound like a Bolshevik."

"I've been reading the newspapers." Lucy began to

laugh along with him. She squeezed his hand so hard he could feel her ring digging into his flesh, almost painfully, like the rim of a stone goblet. "And talking with Doris."

"Oh well, that explains everything." Beaumont drew her towards him and then into his arms. In the next moment he was kissing her, the pink lips soft as flowers, her smell, like mimosa, a distant memory grown suddenly fresh and unutterably real. He closed his eyes. *Denis*, you are a sad man, you always will be, whispered Irène, her doll's eyes glittering. Beaumont pushed the image roughly aside. Lucy was so warm in his arms. He felt the soft shape of her, an ordinary miracle. Tears were starting in the corners of his eyes.

"You're tired out," Lucy murmured. "I should leave you to sleep." She drew away from him slightly, but kept hold of his hands. Beaumont knew she must see his tears, and felt afraid at what she must think of him, but her expression seemed composed entirely of tenderness.

"Don't go," Beaumont said. "Stay with me."

"I do love you, Den. I didn't know what that meant before, not really, but I do now."

"I know."

They lay together on the bed, and although Beaumont was too exhausted to feel more than a vague, undirected pleasure at her physical nearness, he was glad she was there. He reached out with his hands, exploring her face with the tips of his fingers like a blind man, and after a minute or two she began to do the same. It was strange, Beaumont thought, how nearly she seemed a part of him, much more so than she ever had before.

At some point he slept, and he supposed she did, too,

although when he next opened his eyes she was fully awake, standing beside the bed with her clothing straightened and her hair combed in place.

"Doris has supper ready," she said. "Shall we go down?"

There was a hotpot with parsnips and mutton. Doris had prepared a large amount of it, enough to serve the four lodgers who turned out to be currently resident and whose weekly tariff included an evening meal. Beaumont had dreaded these mealtimes without knowing that he did, the invasion of his home and his space by strangers, by foreign bodies. Doris, apparently foreseeing this, served supper to him and Lucy in the kitchen.

"It's warmer in here, anyway," she said. Beaumont sensed she had her eye on them, though for once he seemed unable to guess her thoughts. When the meal was over, Lucy went through to the dining room to help Doris clear away the dishes. Both women seemed adamant that Beaumont should not lift a finger.

"You never finished unpacking," Lucy said, smiling at him in a way that seemed to suggest all manner of things, some of which had already happened, and others that were still to come. Beaumont went upstairs, He hung up his shirts in the wardrobe and slid his suitcase under the bed. He felt a curious sense of disorientation, as if he had set off down one path and then suddenly realised he was proceeding in the wrong direction. He ran a hand over the spines of the books in the bookcase, the novels by Stendhal and Machiavelli, von Clausewitz's great treatise *On War*. The familiar texts, once so cherished, suddenly appeared out of date to him, of the last century, and although he knew he would find it hard to relinquish his fondness for them entirely, he felt certain that if he were to do as Lucy suggested and take up his studies again, he would have to find a different focus.

He thought of Meaulnes, and Alain-Fournier. Ambrose had told him that Alain-Fournier died on the Somme, less than a month after joining up. He remembered what Vladek had said about hunger. He wondered for the hundredth time what had happened to Vladek after they parted.

Beaumont opened the curtains and looked out. Lights blinked in many windows. A taxi drew up at the kerb. After a couple of minutes it drove away. London, Beaumont thought. My Lost Domain.

He went to bed soon afterwards. Some unknowable time later he was awakened by the door opening. He sat up with a jerk, rigid with panic, but then he saw it was only Lucy, Lucy with a light, the planes of her face softly visible in its yellowish glow.

She was wearing a white cotton nightgown. She looked like a ghost.

"Move over," she whispered. She slipped into bed beside him, under the blankets.

"What are you doing?" Beaumont said.

"I thought I'd lost you, Den. I don't want to waste any more time." She shifted her position so she was lying against him, her body pressed close to his along the whole of its length. Beaumont shuddered, the mute force of his arousal gripping his limbs in a paroxysm.

"It's all right," Lucy said. "I want us to. I want to start living our lives." She stroked his head and kissed the corner of his mouth, then eased her hand beneath the elasticated waistband of his pyjamas. Beaumont had found the pyjamas in the top drawer of the tallboy, freshly laundered and neatly folded, a relic from the time before the war. Lucy's fingers brushed his privates, and he experienced a brief, painfully intense vision of the woman with the yellow hair and the awful coat outside Victoria station. He imagined the squalid room she must live in, the greasy pots and pans, the stink of kerosene.

He rolled over on top of Lucy, lifting the white nightgown and rubbing his fingers against her crack. She gasped, though whether in shock or pain or pleasure he did not know. He handled himself, his penis rising immediately to a painful stiffness. He put himself inside Lucy, forcing himself deeper, pressing her back against the sheets, the pure white sheets, so impossible, so familiar, so clean.

Is this what you wanted? he thought. This, and this, and this? Is it?

He opened his eyes. Lucy lay mute beneath him, the milky light of the lamp tainting her face. Her eyes were wide and gleaming, her expression a mixture of bewilderment and forbearance and the determined desire to please. Her fingers touched his hair. She was as lovely as a rose.

"Oh Lucy," Beaumont whispered. "I'm so sorry." Tears were sliding from between his lashes as he began to rock her gently back and forth. He was inside her still, and as he rocked her he felt the blood rising in him again and then he began to fuck her in earnest. He thought of the trees outside, their slim branches pliable as wire, their few remaining leaves encased in shimmering envelopes of ice.

"Lucy," he said, her name sawing in his throat, an inhale and then an exhale, lucy, lucy.

"Den," she said. Her hands gripped his shoulders. Her hair was spread like a sheath of ice across the pillow. She is too lovely, Beaumont thought. He thought of all the women like her who had been turned by the war into just things, into disposable receptacles for men's casual use, or into drying leftovers, their lovers hanging, riddled with bullets, from skeins of barbed wire.

He came with a sensation of falling, as he had almost fallen on the night he had hauled Stephen Lovell out of the mud and into the van. Lucy gripped him with her knees and then went limp. Beaumont lay still for what seemed a long time before he dared look at her. When finally he did, he saw that her eyes were open, gazing up at the ceiling. Light from the lamp danced in orange blotches against the curtains, subdued yet troublesome, like a banked-down furnace.

"Are you all right?" Beaumont said quietly. "I'm sure I must have hurt you. I'm sorry." He found himself unable to say more, to offer her the heartfelt apology he knew she deserved. She turned towards him, her eyes misted, colourless, inscrutable in the semi-darkness.

"You didn't hurt me. It just hurts me to know you're so unhappy. I want us to start again, Den, to start from now."

"Oh Lucy." He rolled on his side, gathering her to him, noticing the way her smell had changed, the sharp prickle of musk beneath the crisp fragrance of washed cotton and lemon soap. "You don't need to start again. Just be who you are. I'm the one that needs to change. And I will, I promise. I'm so glad you waited."

Then she was crying, and he held her. He felt confused and dismayed, his escape route blocked, but at least, he thought, he seemed necessary to her. In Paris he had been necessary to no one. He stroked Lucy's hair, wondering if what she wanted might really be possible. Marriage to Lucy would be no worse a life than many others. He supposed he could try.

"I'm sorry to disturb you," Beaumont said. "Are you Rose Thorpe?"

"I am." The woman looked disconcerted, but not frightened. "Who are you?"

"My name is Dennis Beaumont. I was wondering if I might speak to you for a couple of minutes."

"What's this about?"

"It's about Stephen Lovell. I know I should have written to you first, let you know I was coming. But I wanted to be sure you were still living here." He paused. "It was Stephen who gave me your address."

"Stephen's dead."

As soon as he mentioned Lovell's name, the woman's face seemed to close down, and Beaumont had the sense that she blamed him for Lovell's death, as she must blame everyone who came to the door with any other news than the news she longed for – that there'd been a mistake, that her lover, Stephen Lovell, was alive after all. Yet there was something else there, too – a stark desperation for news of any kind.

"He's dead, yes," said Beaumont quickly. "But he wanted me to bring you his things. He asked me himself." He watched her face carefully for any sign of diminished control, but noticed none. Rose Thorpe was a small woman, not pretty but not plain either. Dark hair hanging loose to her shoulders, slightly flattened, almost oriental features. Her hands were neat and delicate. She wore a ring on her wedding finger, a silver and onyx signet ring

Beaumont guessed had once belonged to Stephen Lovell.

He wondered what she looked like when she smiled. He had Lovell's effects with him in a small cloth bag, which he now thrust forward towards her, wondering if this would be the sum of their meeting, if she would simply snatch the bag from his hands and disappear back inside. Part of him welcomed the idea. The part that had made him decide to come here in the first place hoped there would be more.

Beaumont realised he wanted to talk about Lovell, if only to make this woman understand that he had tried to save him.

"Could I come in, just for a moment?" he said. "It doesn't seem right, somehow, talking about him here on the street."

She reached out to touch the bag then took a rapid couple of steps backward into the hallway. Beaumont followed. The hallway was dingy, furnished with dark green wallpaper and a faded red stair runner. The wallpaper was beginning to come away from the wall in places. The house was in Croydon, in a side street that was also dingy, and where most of the properties had been divided into smaller flats. Rose Thorpe's flat was at the back of the house, two rooms and an outside privy. The main room had been divided by a curtain to make a living room and bedroom. The second room, the kitchen, was long and narrow, dominated by an enormous cast iron stove and an old Welsh dresser, its shelves crammed with books. The stove was lit, but the flat had a chilly, spartan feel nonetheless that reminded Beaumont of his room in Paris. How treacherous life was, that it was he who was here now with Rose and not Stephen Lovell. He wondered if Lovell had thought of these rooms at the end, if he had been able to think of anything, other than his own agony and the stink of his shit.

"How well did you know Stephen?" Rose said. She made him tea, serving it in a blue and white willow-pattern beaker with a chipped rim and no saucer. Beaumont could tell she was trying to be brave, trying to ask reasonable questions when in fact no reasonable answers to those questions existed.

If she thought he was going to tell her anything outside of the bare facts, she was wrong.

"I didn't really know him at all," Beaumont said. "Or only for a couple of hours. I drove the ambulance that brought him in. Everything possible was done to save him, but he had lost too much blood."

"But you were with him when he died?"

Beaumont nodded. "He asked me to give you these." He handed her the cloth bag. "There isn't much, I'm afraid. Just the things he had with him. I don't know what happened to the rest of his possessions."

"The army sent them back to his family." She paused. "Was he in much pain?"

"A little. But it didn't last long."

"I don't want you to lie to me."

Yes, you do, Beaumont thought. "I'm not lying," he said. "He lost consciousness fairly quickly. That's what happens with blood loss."

She continued to stare at him, trying to hold his gaze with her chalky blue eyes. He took another swallow of his tea.

"How was he able to tell you where I lived if he was unconscious?" Rose said.

"That was before."

"What else did he tell you? Before he lost consciousness?"

"Nothing. Just that he wanted me to find you and give you his papers. That was all he talked about. I wish I could tell you more, but there's nothing to tell."

She nodded slowly. Beaumont could not tell if she believed him or not. "I'm sorry if I've been discourteous, Mr Beaumont," she said. "It's just that it's been very difficult, trying to find out the truth of what happened to him. Stephen's family won't tell me anything – they didn't even invite me to his memorial service. We weren't married, you see." She smiled a cold smile. "In the end you don't know what to believe, so you believe nothing."

"I would say that's a healthy attitude to have, especially when it comes to the war," Beaumont said. He realised he liked this woman. In her intelligence and plain way of speaking she reminded him a little of Doris, although she was older than Doris, from the look of her, thirty at least. Stephen Lovell, he knew from his papers, had been twenty-five. Beaumont had no doubt Rose had been badly treated by Lovell's family, but what of her own family? He wondered what chain of events had brought her to this poky suburban flat. "Why don't you tell me something about Stephen?" he said at last. He already knew that Stephen Lovell had faced his end with considerable bravery and a minimum of fuss. Beaumont had no particular wish to know more – he couldn't see the point in it – but if talking about her lover made Rose Thorpe forget her questions about his death then that was point enough.

"I'm not sure what to say," Rose said. She put down her own cup, a white porcelain teacup with a faded gold rim. "We hadn't known each other all that long, you see, not really. I met him at a concert, during one of his leaves. One of the composers on the programme was a friend of Stephen's, from university. He wanted Stephen to write something for him, something about the war that he could set to music. Stephen said he'd think about it. He told the friend he didn't know much about opera but the friend said that didn't matter, it was Stephen's words he wanted."

"Stephen was a poet, then?"

"Oh no. He wrote for the newspapers. About the war, mostly, and how much he disapproved of it. He felt he had to join up, to see the war for himself, or he'd never be able to write truthfully about it. That was Stephen – always dashing around after the truth. His father wanted him to be a lawyer, but he was having none of it. We did plan on getting married when the war was over, because we knew it would make our lives simpler, but it didn't seem important, not to us. I did love him, and I think he loved me. I still can't quite believe he's dead, but I think that's because it happened so far away."

She rose to her feet and took her cup over to the sink. It took a moment for Beaumont to realise she was crying.

"I'm sorry," she said. "I expect you've been dreading this."

"No," he said, then stopped, because he had been, most of all what he was seeing now – her tears. Now the moment had come he felt ashamed – ashamed that he didn't have the courage or the callousness to tell her about the frightful and degrading way her lover had died. He stood up, thinking he should leave, and then sat down again. It came to him that this was the last he would see of this woman, and felt overcome with regret. It was as if they had shared something important – as if they were still sharing it. He did not like the thought of leaving her alone in these dismal rooms. He wanted to tell her that he had read Lovell's papers, or diaries, or whatever they were, that Lovell had not given up on his mission to discredit the war, that she should know that, whatever.

But what if she turned on him, angry that he had presumed to pry into the secrets Lovell had entrusted to his care? Words that had been meant for her alone? Even though it was not true – as a journalist, Lovell would surely have intended his writings to be consumed and understood by as many readers as possible – he could hardly blame her if she interpreted his curiosity as a betrayal.

"I'll leave you my address," he said instead. "In case you need anything." He searched his pockets for a scrap of paper, and when he was unable to find one, Rose handed him an old envelope that had been lying face-down on the kitchen table and told him he could write on the back of that.

"Thank you for coming," she said. She smiled again, a proper smile this time. It transformed her face. "You've helped me a great deal. I really mean that." She put out her hand for him to shake, and as he took it he wondered what might happen if he asked Rose Thorpe to go away to Paris with him. Such thoughts were insane, Beaumont thought, though no more insane than the thought of letting them go unspoken. He left soon after, worried that he might do something foolish, something irrevocable. He missed his way heading back to the station and ended up walking the three miles to the next stop along the line.

He ate lunch in the station buffet at Victoria,

absentmindedly scanning the crowds for the woman in the blue chenille coat.

He found her, three weeks later, in The Commoner's Arms, a pub not far from where he went drinking with Dickie Ferguson on the day he returned from Paris. The woman in the blue coat was employed as a barmaid there. Her name was Elizabeth Drew.

"It's Billie," she said. "No one ever called me Elizabeth except my schoolteachers."

"I like Billie better," Beaumont said. He was fascinated by her voice, her inconsistent attempts to hide her broad South London vowels beneath a careless layering-on of shabby-genteel. He wondered who she thought she was fooling. "Where were you born, then, Billie?"

"Richmond," Billie said. "Upon Thames."

Battersea, more like, Beaumont thought. He laughed. She reminded him tantalisingly of Irène, although of course she looked nothing like her. Billie was ten years older at least, and although her face still held the cast of her former beauty it was faint, more like a memory than the real thing. Beaumont supposed she reminded him of the French waitress because both women pretended to be something they weren't. Irène liked to imagine herself as an artist's model. Billie still believed she would be 'discovered', that a rich man would one day take a fancy to her and bestow on her all the material luxuries she saw as rightfully hers.

Billie's fantasies should have made her pathetic, but Beaumont found them touching. He admired Billie's courage in sustaining a fantasy life at all. He took to visiting Billie on her evenings off. She lived above the bar, sharing the privy and the kitchen facilities with the pub landlord and his family. There was always a fire burning, at least when Beaumont was there, favouring her mean apartment with an atmosphere of comfort and warmth he found unexpectedly relaxing. Rose Thorpe's flat had not felt half so pleasant to be in, in spite of the books and the kitchen stove and Rose herself. Billie was especially fond of pretty trinkets, and these were everywhere about: cheap souvenirs of European spa towns, a type of coloured glassware that Beaumont found particularly hideous, lacquered wooden matchbox covers, ceramic animals.

"Where do you find all this stuff?" Beaumont asked her once. Most of the objects were worthless and many were ugly, but they fascinated him, nonetheless, perhaps because in some small measure they reminded him of the silver napkin ring he had found in the ashes of the ruined farmhouse in Cassaron. Without saying a word to Lucy or Doris, he had bought a canister of metal polish and cleaned the silver, removing every fleck and strap of tarnish from the intricate chasing. What lay beneath turned out to be a hunting scene, a design showing a fox being pursued by a pack of hounds. Each hound was rendered in detail, but the fox was like a shadow, a were-thing, a blank space where a fox might have been.

There was a hallmark on the inside of the ring, a horizontal line of four stamped symbols that Beaumont knew would identify the place and date of manufacture, perhaps even the name of the engraver, a code that could be broken quite easily given access to the appropriate books. Beaumont supposed he should make the effort, but he held back, nonetheless. It seemed to him that the napkin ring was in its own way a distillation of everything that could ever be known about the lives of people in Europe before the war, not just the lives of the family who owned it but of their neighbours and their neighbours' neighbours, matters important and trivial, public and private.

A part of Beaumont believed the ring should be allowed to keep its secrets. He wondered if Billie, in her own way, felt similarly about the gaudy trash on her mantelpiece, and supposed she must do. What purpose was served by such things, if not to keep the past alive and keep it present?

"Here and there," Billie said. "The glass was my mother's, she used to collect it. Carnival glass, it's called. I buy the odd cup and saucer myself down the Portobello Road if it grabs my fancy. Some of the punters give me stuff, too. There was a gent in here the other week." Her face took on a dreamy look. "I don't mean he was in here as in, *in this room*," she added hurriedly, although Beaumont knew he probably had been. It was no secret to him that Billie liked men in her life. So far as Beaumont was concerned, her promiscuity only made her more attractive. "He was in a few times, actually. Had a foreign accent. Some of the regulars used to go on about him being a German spy, but you know what those jokers are like, they'd claim their own mothers were German spies if they'd had enough beers. This fellow was a gentleman, wouldn't hurt a fly. His coat was all in patches, I remember, so I suppose he was short of a bob or two. That's the war for you though, isn't it? Anyway, he gave me this." She indicated one of the china figurines that crowded the mantel shelf, a harlequin, leaning against a tree stump and with a goblet of ale clasped in one outstretched hand. The glaze coating the little man's face was seen to be cracked in several places, and Beaumont felt chilled suddenly, in spite of the fire. He could not help thinking of the scarred veteran he had seen on the day he returned from Paris. He rose from his seat and crossed to the fireplace. There was no doubt that the harlequin was beautifully made – of a much higher quality than Billie's other trinkets – but Beaumont found there was something sinister about it, nonetheless. Most likely it was the thing's mouth, red-lipped and fiendishly grinning, or maybe its face, which was white, expressionless, the face of a clown in full greasepaint. Whatever it was, Beaumont thought there was something devilish about it, something malign. He turned it over to look at the base. The maker's mark, two crossed swords, stirred a memory. He had an idea the figure might be Meissen.

"I'd be careful with this if I were you," Beaumont said. "I think it might be worth something."

"Well, if it turns out to make my fortune, I'll cut you in," Billie said. "I'm rather fond of the little fellow, actually. I intend on keeping him. What makes you so interested all of a sudden?"

"I'm not. He's an ugly little brute, if you ask me."

"Each to his own, I say. Now, are you going to spend the whole evening pontificating about the price of fish, or what?" She let down her hair, tugging it free of the pins she used to keep it off her face when she was working in the bar. Beaumont thought what he always thought at such moments: that he had to stop seeing her, that their relationship was dangerous precisely because there was so little point to it, that what he gained was out of all proportion to what he risked. If he had felt any genuine affection for Billie, things might have been different. As it was, what he felt was mainly a fascination with his own fascination.

Billie's feelings, whatever they were, were of little account to him.

In the moments before they had sex, Beaumont liked to imagine Billie as he had first seen her, stooping down to get into the taxi, her soft, bulky body wrapped in the grubby folds of the blue chenille-looking coat. He had searched for the coat in Billie's rooms, but never seen it. Neither did he dare ask her about it, in case she got hold of the idea he had been spying on her.

So far as Billie was concerned they had met by chance, when Beaumont happened to drop into The Commoner's Arms for a pint of bitter.

The falsity of her assumption, the murky interplay of chance and destiny, was something he found arousing. Billie shook her head, making her heavy, brass-coloured hair switch about her face, and as always Beaumont thought of a carthorse shaking its mane to rid itself of flies.

Her arse and thighs were broad, like a Percheron's, the flesh puckered and lightly traced with bluish-green veins.

Beaumont took her from behind, bending her across the bed, his left hand gripping and twisting her meaty left breast. He would have liked to penetrate her anus, but so far at least she had not let him. He contented himself with fingering the aperture of that orifice, chafing the ball of his thumb on the stiffly curled golden hairs that grew out of it. Billie groaned. Beaumont drove himself deep inside her, causing the further edge of the iron bed frame to bump noisily against the wall. His orgasm was sudden and intense. Afterwards, as always, he felt broken and tired. He made his escape as soon as he could, telling Billie there were business matters he should attend to. Apart from his name he had given her almost no personal information about himself. Billie knew he had been at the Front, but little more. Beaumont had the feeling she liked it that way, that his maintaining a mystery about himself enabled her to mould her idea of him to suit her fantasies. This knowledge disturbed him, but aside from breaking with Billie he could see no way of confronting the issue.

The outside air was chilly, with a hint of rain. After the stuffiness of Billie's rooms, the cold came as a relief. Beaumont headed due south from Victoria, making his way through the back streets of Pimlico until he came to the river. He did not hurry. It was not yet nine o'clock, and he was in no rush to get home. Since the first week of his homecoming, matters had grown increasingly difficult between himself and Lucy. The problems had so far not expressed themselves in open conflict, but rather as a distance between them, together with a lessening of the trust and intimacy Lucy had allowed him in those first few days. It seemed that Lucy's nocturnal visit to his room had been a singular occurrence. She told Beaumont she didn't like the idea of the lodgers gossiping.

"They know we're not married," she said. "Everyone knows we're not married." The question buried inside her statement was clear, but for Beaumont it became a question he felt increasingly reluctant to respond to. There was no doubt in his mind that Lucy had changed beyond all expectations. In her enthusiasm for her new business venture and her competence in dealing with all matters arising from it, Beaumont found Lucy reminding him more and more of her father. He wondered guiltily if it were this new self confidence that made him hesitate, if he had secretly liked having her helpless and selfish, so he could feel comfortable and comforted in his own moral and intellectual superiority.

He knew he could not say for certain but he doubted it. It was true that he felt disconcerted at having to constantly re-evaluate his attitudes regarding Lucy, but at the same time his respect for her as a human being had increased substantially. Also she was beautiful. Beaumont could find no reason he could easily identify not to marry Lucy, not to set a date for their wedding as soon as possible, yet still he hesitated. Their one sexual encounter still haunted him. Lucy had not remained in his bed that night, and although she seemed calm the following morning, happy even, Beaumont wondered if a fragment of the new distance between them had been lodged inside her smile, even then.

Also, there was Rose Thorpe. Ever since his visit to her flat in Croydon, Beaumont found himself dwelling more and more on the crazy thought that had come into his mind while he was there, that he should ask Stephen Lovell's lover to run away with him. He barely knew the woman, and yet he could not rid himself of the sense that they were close in some way. There were times when his mind felt raw with its awareness of her, even though so far as he was aware she had made no attempt to contact him. On some days he felt certain she would write to him, even if only to try and extract further information about the death of Stephen Lovell. When no letter came, Beaumont tormented himself with the thought that she might have lost the scrap of envelope with his address on, and so would not be able to get in touch with him, even if she wanted to.

He could go and see her any day he wanted to, yet

held back from doing so, fearing he might make a fool of himself in some unforeseen but disastrous way.

He knew his visits to Billie had more to do with his Rose obsession than with his confusion over Lucy.

He walked across Vauxhall Bridge and down into Kennington Lane. It was gone ten by his watch. Somewhere a fox barked. The sound made him jump, as all sudden, loud or unusual sounds still did. At the Front, any unexpected noise could mean danger or death. Beaumont carried on up the road, hurrying now, fighting the conviction that what he had heard had not been a fox but a man, screaming from the pain of his wounds. Even wounds that had begun to heal sometimes turned septic and filled up with pus. Wounds that had not hurt at first sometimes became a torture so great they erased the person that had sustained them, even before he died.

His friend Ambrose Weston told him he'd once had to shoot a man who had sustained a groin injury.

"He begged me, and there was no one else who would do it, so I did," Ambrose said. "I feel it's the most important thing I've ever done."

Beaumont wondered how Ambrose had squared that with his religion. Beaumont had never once thought of shooting Stephen Lovell, even though it was clear almost from the first that he would not survive. He knew it was notoriously difficult to kill a man with a single bullet. He imagined himself firing shot after shot into Lovell, blasting new wounds on top of the old, the man tied to a living hell by a thread that refused to break. His palms broke out in sweat, and when the fox barked again his heart began to hammer in his chest.

Was this Lovell, haunting him? Did Lovell somehow

know about his feelings for Rose? For a second he thought unaccountably of the china harlequin on Billie's mantelpiece, the red, vaguely snarling lips, the mask for a face.

There are demons on the battlefield, he thought. Everyone knows that. He had no idea where the words arose from, but as he came in sight of the house he seemed to see a figure emerge from the side passage and head off up the road. The figure was stout, with a long coat that reached down almost to its ankles.

The orange light from the streetlamp glanced off its back. Its coat appeared to be patched in several places.

It's evil, he thought, and this time the words were Lovell's, writing about the war. In the diaries Beaumont had given to Rose, Lovell had written about his belief that the war was not the result of a sickness already present in society, as some of the newspapers seemed to think, but an evil inflicted on the ordinary citizen by industrialists and politicians, eager to turn the slaughter to their advantage. Beaumont thought it had probably been Lovell's anger about the war that kept him alive as far as the farmhouse. Lovell had lost so much blood by the time Beaumont found him that Beaumont knew he should already be dead.

Vladek had placed his hand in Lovell's wound, trying to close it from the inside, but after a couple of minutes he had shaken his head.

"This man is finished," he said. His hands were red to the wrists, as if he were wearing gloves.

"He'll hear you," Beaumont had said. Vladek shook his head, wiping both hands on the skirts of his overcoat. The overcoat was patched in several places. The next time Beaumont looked down at Lovell, he was dead.

There were still lights on in the downstairs windows. Beaumont crept towards the gate, slowly, as if fearful of being apprehended. Before he had the chance to use his key, Doris opened the door from the inside.

"Where have you been?" she said. It was unlike Doris to question him. He wondered what she would say if he told her the truth.

"Just walking," Beaumont said. "I heard a fox."

She stared at him. "Lucy's gone to bed. She has to be at the bank first thing in the morning. Do you want anything to eat?"

"I ate dinner at a pub." Billie's corned beef hash, which was greasy and mostly potato but it filled him up. Doris nodded, then told him Dickie Ferguson was dead.

"He shot himself," she said. "He was supposed to have handed his gun back, but he didn't."

Beaumont had met up with Ferguson two weeks previously, once again more by chance than from volition. The stubble grew thickly on Ferguson's cheeks, the scar on his face running through it like a red river through a copse of stunted trees.

"I think I'm going to lose my job," Ferguson said. He told Beaumont that Westcombe's new headmaster had taken against him, but Beaumont sensed there was more to it. He remembered the way Ferguson had squeezed his shoulder outside the King James on his first day back, and supposed Ferguson had got himself into trouble over some boy.

Ferguson was drinking whisky and his eyes were bloodshot. Beaumont thought of Billie, her ample form crouched low over the bed, and wondered how far things had gone with Ferguson before he was found out.

Beaumont felt sick with fatigue. He said goodnight to Doris and then went to his room. He stopped briefly outside Lucy's door, wondering if he should knock and deciding not to. He wondered where the fox was, where beneath the whole dark blanket of the London night it made its home.

People call it a bark, but it's really a cry, he thought. One of the patches on Vladek's coat had been a bright fox orange.

Beaumont had written a brief note to his supervisor at Magdalen while he was still in Paris, telling him he didn't know when or if he would be returning to complete his dissertation. Edwin Martingale had written back, informing Beaumont that if he thought he could assuage the guilt of nations by sacrificing his personal ambitions he was being a fool. Beaumont read and reread the letter several times, but did not reply to it. He had always admired Martingale because he was arrogant, demanding, and never seemed to give a damn how many enemies he made, but he was not in any mood to be persuaded. A month after his return to London, Beaumont wrote to Martingale again, saying he was thinking of changing the subject of his thesis. Martingale replied by return, stating that if Beaumont was serious, he should come up at the earliest opportunity so they could discuss the matter face to face.

Martingale's note was brief but caustically witty, a sure sign that the professor was pleased to hear from him. He also offered Beaumont the use of his spare room if he took it into his head to stay overnight. Martingale had occupied the same set of rooms at Magdalen for thirty years, and

Beaumont's memories of Oxford were in a sense indivisible from his memories of Martingale's rooms, with their pervasive aromas of book dust and Virginia tobacco.

The day Beaumont travelled up to Oxford it was raining. As he walked east along the High towards Magdalen Bridge, he thought how the brief eighteen months of his studentship not only seemed long distant, but part of another life entirely. The students he glimpsed – on bicycles, through the misted windows of public houses, standing together in loquacious, cheerful-sounding groups in the college gateways – looked not just young, but unknowing, their faces unmarked by carnage or any idea of war save what they might have gleaned from the newspapers. Beaumont envied them, yet he despised them, too. He could not imagine how he might communicate with them.

The faces of his coevals, those he might have approached with a sense of mutual understanding, were conspicuous only by their absence.

They never came back, that's why, Beaumont thought. They're all dead. As he stared at the arrangement of academic gowns and college scarves in the polished, brightly lit windows of Shepherd and Woodward, the university outfitter, it came to him that the whole of Oxford had become a display case, a museum exhibit, a kind of bricks-and-mortar reconstruction of Alain-Fournier's idea of the Lost Domain. He felt overcome by a sense of vertigo, the destructive circularity of his thought processes wearing away at his mind, like a new form of cancer. He kept thinking of a poem he had once read, something about not being able to swim in the same river twice. He wished he could remember who it was by. Most of all, he was overwhelmed by the conviction that his original instincts had been correct, that it was too late for him, that the war had destroyed the possibility of a return to this place more surely and more wantonly than if mortar shells had physically torn apart the parks and buildings and cloisters of Magdalen College.

He remembered the letter Martingale had sent him while he was in France, castigating him for giving up his chances. The letter had spoken to him at least – if not for that letter he would never have come back here – and it occurred to Beaumont that if he could only talk to the professor about how he felt, honestly and without restraint, then there was at least a chance he might be able to overcome his anxieties and reclaim his life. Martingale was not like the new young students, he would perhaps understand something of what Beaumont was feeling. Most importantly Martingale would see the war differently. Not as something he himself had experienced, that was true, but as a phenomenon whose potency might eventually become dulled by time, its status reassigned to that of an unpleasant memory.

But when Beaumont presented himself at the porter's lodge, the man behind the desk informed him that he could not see Edwin Martingale, because Edwin Martingale was dead.

"A heart attack, they say. Happened two days ago." The man paused, and wiped his nose with the back of his hand. He was stout, buttressed against the weather by a regular and committed intake of the local real ale. "You're looking a bit green, sir, if you don't mind my saying so. Can I bring you a cup of tea? A sandwich, maybe? Wouldn't take a tick."

"No, thank you," Beaumont said. He shook his head

and turned away, not wanting the porter to see he was on the verge of tears. "I'll write to the bursar," he said at last. His voice caught in his throat, like a splinter. He walked away before the porter could question him further. He headed back to the High, unsure of which direction he should take. He wondered what would happen if he carried on walking east, out of Oxford and into Headington. He could stay the night at a roadside inn and check out the following morning as a different person.

He caught a glimpse of this other-self, going door to door selling vacuum cleaners, or working in the kitchens of a hospital or a prison in Manchester or Birmingham. Those possible-lives felt real where his own did not. His whole body felt heavy with grief, though whether the grief was for Martingale or Dickie Ferguson or for himself he hardly knew.

The rain had slackened off. Rays of lemon-yellow sunshine filtered through the dispersing clouds like the beams of pale searchlights. The granite pavements sparkled with mica. Beaumont breathed deeply, thinking how differently the rain smelled here from the rain at the Front. At the Front, the rain was always tainted by the reek of ashes and rusting metal. Here it smelled of earth and new spring grass. He headed west towards Carfax, stopping off at the covered market to buy souvenirs for Lucy and for Doris. He stood for some time in front of a stall selling antique jewellery, wondering what he might buy for Rose Thorpe and finally buying nothing at all. When he arrived at the station he found the London train had recently left, that there was the better part of an hour to wait until the next one. He went to the station buffet, where he purchased a cup of milky tea and a ham sandwich. He took a seat near the window, wishing he had something to read other than the battered copy of Machiavelli's *The Prince* he had brought to discuss with Martingale. Beaumont had come to distrust *The Prince*, a text he had once worshipped as the most devout kind of truth-telling, but which he now saw increasingly as a brilliantly irrelevant abstraction, a diagram of the way power flowed, precise and logical as a drawing by Da Vinci and equally confined to the same two basic dimensions.

The war he had seen on the ground had not been like that. For the men who had to fight in it, the Prince's elegant struggle for power was a welter of chaos. Machiavelli's thesis was a thing of beauty, but it was not the whole truth.

Beaumont rested the book on his knees and stared out of the window, watching the people coming and going on the platform and reflecting that the thing he had always liked most about cities was that he himself could come and go without being noticed. In that respect Oxford, like London, provided the ideal refuge for the unquiet mind.

Goodbye, old man, he thought. He wished he had responded more fully to Martingale's last letter. He found himself wondering what would now happen to Martingale's collection of Meerschaum pipes. So far as Beaumont knew, Martingale had no relatives, no one close, anyway. He wished he'd asked the porter when Martingale's funeral was to be. Still, it was too late now.

Eventually the train arrived. Beaumont went to the front, which was always less crowded, and was pleased to find he had a compartment to himself. The train's whistle expelled a shriek as the brakes were released. At the same moment a man emerged from the ticket office and came dashing in leaping strides towards the platform's edge.

Beaumont rose from his seat in alarm, thinking he meant to throw himself beneath the wheels. When he saw the man was intent only on catching the train, he relaxed a little, but his relief was short-lived – the increasing speed of the train combined with the lunatic's inability to match it made it look as if he stood a good chance of ending up on the rails anyway. Beaumont stared at the man in horror and amazement as he put on a sudden burst of speed, bringing his face almost level with Beaumont's at the carriage window. His teeth were bared, and he seemed to be grinning, although Beaumont guessed his features were merely twisted from the exertion of running.

His coat, which appeared to be patched in several places, flapped out behind him like a coarse grey sail. It's going to get caught in the wheels, Beaumont thought. He watched, mesmerised, as the lunatic leapt forward, seizing the door handle of the carriage and wrenching it downwards. Beaumont knew that what he was seeing was impossible, that no man could run that fast, but the awful spectacle continued to happen. The carriage door swung open, blocking Beaumont's view of what was happening on the platform. There was a loud thump, and for one horrifying moment he felt convinced the man had been flung beneath the train after all, but a second later the door was slammed closed from the inside. The platform flew to an end. Someone was cursing loudly in the corridor. Beaumont went to his compartment door and peered out. His heart was hammering. Suddenly the man's face loomed up before him on the other side of the glass. Beaumont stepped rapidly backwards and almost fell over.

The man was Vladek.

The compartment door flew open.

"Damned train left three minutes early," Vladek said. "Do you mind if I share your compartment?"

Beaumont sat down with a thump.

"What were you doing?" he said faintly. "You could have been killed."

"Occupational hazard, I'm afraid. I'm always running late. It's a habit I can't seem to break." He thrust out his hand, the long fingers, slightly swollen at the knuckles, that Beaumont had seen reaching into the sticky blackness of Lovell's wound. The fingernails were clean now, polished as pearls. Beaumont reached out and grasped his hand, watching in disbelief as his own fingers folded around Vladek's, tugging them downwards in a brief, tense handshake. He released Vladek's hand, part of him still doubting its concrete reality. Vladek began to unbutton his coat.

"Why are you here?" Beaumont said.

"I'm sorry," Vladek said. "Have we met?" He spoke exactly as Beaumont remembered, the same trace of accent, the soft inflection of sibilants masking harder vowels.

"You know we've met. Near Cassaron. It was the night Lovell died. You drove my ambulance out of no-man's-land." He paused. "You probably saved my life."

Vladek hung up his coat and sat down. He settled himself against the cushions then leaned back in his seat, his arms folded lightly against his chest.

"My memory is not the best," he said at last. "You'll have to forgive me." He smiled briefly, exposing his teeth. "I don't recall the incident, but if I was of help to you in some way I am pleased to hear it." Beaumont fell silent. He felt himself brimming with the same sensation of unbelief as when the porter on the gate of Magdalen College told him the man he had come to see no longer existed. It seemed obvious that Vladek was lying. Why he was lying was less clear. To see what Beaumont would do, most likely. Like anyone confronted with a lie, he could choose either to confront the liar or go along with the fiction. He remembered the disfigured veteran in the King James pub, the man in the long coat he had seen on Kennington Lane the night Doris told him Dickie Ferguson had killed himself. Beaumont had mistaken both these men for Vladek, however briefly, but he knew that *this* was not a mistake. Now that Vladek was here in front of him, Beaumont understood he had assumed that Vladek was dead. The way Vladek was sitting – his head thrown back, the casually crossed arms – seemed actively to invite scrutiny, and so Beaumont stared, at the pallor of Vladek's face, the high, sculpted cheekbones, the scattering of pockmarks, like scars left by acid, across his right cheek. His lashes were transparent and very sparse. His silver-grey eyes gleamed wetly, like the eyes of a fish. Beaumont felt very alive suddenly, the way he sometimes had at the Front, at Cassaron even. He had not expected to feel like that again.

"Well, I'm glad you made it back," he said to Vladek, his words as slippery and non-committal as Vladek's own.

"You were at Cassaron, you say? I heard the whole place went up in smoke." He paused. "What were you doing in Oxford?"

"I was supposed to be meeting with my supervisor. I've been thinking about coming back to complete my thesis."

"How did it go? The meeting, I mean?"

"It didn't. The man I came to see has just died of a heart attack."

"And no one wrote to tell you?" Vladek raised an eyebrow. The eyebrow, like his eyelashes, was almost colourless.

"I expect the college had other things to think about. And knowing Martingale, I doubt he wrote down the appointment anyway."

"And you cared for this man, Martingale?"

"I cared about him, yes." Beaumont paused. Vladek's question – personal, direct and not a little intrusive – seemed to sum up everything he had learned about the man in the brief time he had known him. If he had harboured any doubts about Vladek's identity, his question about Edwin Martingale would have banished them in a second.

On the night of Lovell's death, Beaumont and Vladek sat in the ambulance behind the ruined farmhouse and talked together until dawn. As soon as it was light, Vladek jumped down and trudged off along the muddy track that led between the burned-out cowsheds and back towards the main road. He told Beaumont he was going to have a look at the road, but he had never returned, and a short while later Beaumont had caught sight of a British convoy, heading eastwards towards what remained of Cassaron. When the CO asked Beaumont the number of his unit, Beaumont gave it.

"I lost them in the dark somehow," Beaumont said. "Any idea where they've got to?"

The CO shook his head. "That unit's gone," he said. "You'd better tag along with us for the time being."

Beaumont followed in the wake of the trucks, through a wasteland of ruins that just three days previously had been a lively market town with a *café central* and a *hotel de ville*, a busy market square, surrounded by neat flint and stone cottages. The rubble was still smouldering. A dog with an injured hind leg scurried back and forth along the fifty yards of cobbled street that remained, miraculously undamaged, in front of the *mairie*. One of the men shot the dog, and the CO bawled him out for wasting ammunition. Beaumont thought of Lovell, whom they had left behind in the barn, his body covered with a mildewed piece of sacking. Even though Beaumont knew better, he kept worrying that Lovell might not be dead, that he would awaken to discover he had been abandoned. He kept wanting to go back, to be sure.

He tried not to think about Vladek. That Vladek was now here, safe in the railway carriage and asking him about Martingale, seemed both fantastic and ordinary, the most normal thing that had happened to him since his return.

"Martingale had a fine mind, but the world as he understood it has been destroyed," Beaumont said. "The old order ended at Cassaron. I wouldn't have known how to talk to him about that, how to explain it. Perhaps it's just as well he died before I could try."

"For your sake, or for his? If he had a fine mind, as you say, do you not think he may have found the world as it is more interesting than the world that has gone?"

"Perhaps, but I doubt it. Martingale was interested in ideas. The only idea at Cassaron was to reduce it to rubble."

"The same idea we saw at Carthage, then, or Antioch, or Constantinople. The whole of history is a series of witch-burnings. Cassaron was no different. The world soon recovers."

Beaumont fell silent. The letter Martingale sent him in Paris seemed to suggest that it was not war that was important so much as war's aftermath. *You have suffered an atrocity*, Martingale wrote. *But what defines a man is what he makes of himself in spite of that. Not what is enacted upon him, but how he reacts.* Beaumont had come to Oxford prepared to argue that war was different when one witnessed it first hand, that the very fact of war demanded a change in one's way of thinking. That a life lived in denial of that was a half-life, a betrayal of what you had witnessed and the men who had died.

He had expected Martingale to argue against him, to chivvy him back to his old life with all its comfortable, explicable priorities. Beaumont knew he had come to Oxford for precisely that reason: to vent his anger and then to be given permission to put it away, to return to his studies unhindered by guilt, with the sense that he was doing a brave thing instead of a cowardly thing. But hearing these same arguments from the mouth of Vladek, who had also been at Cassaron and so knew the truth of it, made Beaumont uneasy. He could not escape the idea that Vladek was trying to catch him out somehow, to trick him into abandoning even those shreds of half-certainties he had glimpsed as Lovell lay dying. Beaumont did not know the meaning of what he had seen, and understood still less of what he was supposed to do with that knowledge once he had gained it. He knew only that continuing in the old way should be – must be – impossible.

He glanced down at his copy of *The Prince*, lying all but forgotten on the seat beside him. Vladek, a paler likeness of the etching by Goya that adorned the cover, saw him doing it, and smiled. Beaumont felt he would have smiled the same smile at the veteran with the shattered face, at Dickie Ferguson, who had blown his brains out with his service weapon for the love of a boy.

He would have smiled the same smile in the ruins of Cassaron. *Let's cook up some horsemeat and talk things over. So long as we're alive, that's the thing, isn't it, my brother?*

"How did you get out?" Beaumont said suddenly.

"I walked. A long distance, but I found my way eventually. You are looking well, by the way. I'm glad you made it." He reached into the pocket of his coat and drew out a book, a well worn volume missing its cover. He began to read. Beaumont sat gazing out of the window. Even though they were silent they were still talking, Vladek and he, it was the farmhouse at Cassaron all over again, the farmhouse would always be there, no matter what happened and even if he never saw Vladek again after today. He glanced at Vladek, his head bent calmly over his book. For all his pallor, he seemed to Beaumont to be composed entirely of darkness.

Suddenly and from nowhere he thought of Rose Thorpe. The idea of her, like a still point inside him, made him feel less afraid.

Vladek did not speak again until they were pulling into Paddington station. As the train drew alongside the platform he pulled on his coat and stuffed the book back into his pocket. "It was good to see you again," he said. He tugged open the compartment door and went out into the corridor. "Mind how you go."

He stepped from the train on to the platform. Beaumont followed, but more slowly. He watched as Vladek strode away from him, growing smaller with distance, the patches on his coat like the coloured squares of a Mondrian painting: gunmetal blue, Prussian green, foxfire orange. Eventually the crowd swallowed him completely, and Beaumont found himself having to resist the urge to run after him, to grab him by the arm and speak his name, simply to prove to himself that Vladek had actually been there in the first place.

My first task was learning to drive. I had never experienced the desire to own a motor car previously, and so had not learned to handle one. I was taught by a man named Raymond Winston, who for reasons I never discovered was known as Ted. Ted was over fifty, a parts engineer who had lost a foot in an accident with a steam hammer. He had a wooden prosthesis. When he'd had a few beers, Ted would detach his wooden foot and pass it around as if it were a trophy he'd been awarded. Like a trophy it was engraved with names, initials and expletives, the signatures of the men who worked with Ted in engineering.

Ted was an expert in his job, but he never talked about his personal life. Everything I came to know about him I learned from others. I wasn't at the base long, but I came to enjoy the routine. From Ted I learned how to strip down and fine-tune an engine. I took a pride in the work, because it seemed clear to me that the skills I was learning could prove useful, not just for the war effort but afterwards. In the evenings I read.

There were rumours that the Channel had been mined. Many of our lads had never travelled abroad before. Some had never even seen the sea. They seemed excited and afraid in equal measures. By then I felt confident in the work I had been trained to do. I had also become curious about what war might be like first hand. The idea that any of our company might actually be killed was still far from my mind, a theory, like the speed of light, that you have heard explained but forget the rudiments of almost immediately.

Most of the men I trained with were killed in less than three months. I remember Sergeant Nigel Seward, who first introduced me to the card game, Anne Boleyn. Each game consisted of four rounds. In each round, a different suit of cards - hearts, clubs, diamonds and then spades - became the trump suit. Each trump card carried points according to its face value. All non-trump cards were points-neutral, excepting the Queen of Spades, which always carried fifty points, regardless of whether spades was the trump suit. The aim of the game was to *not* accrue points. To win at Anne Boleyn, you had to remember which cards had already been played, and dump your highest-scoring cards as soon as you could. To win a trick early on in the game was not usually dangerous, and was often desirable as it meant you could keep control over which suit had the lead. As the game progressed, however, it was better to force the lead on to someone else. The player holding the Queen of Spades would always want to rid himself of trump cards as quickly as possible, so he could drop the queen on whoever still had trumps in his hand.

When you played the Queen of Spades, it was customary to shout: 'off with her head!'

Nigel Seward was obsessed with Anne Boleyn. He had a near-photographic memory, and an uncanny knack of knowing who held which cards, even when the game was scarcely begun. Beating Seward at Anne Boleyn acquired a certain cachet. Gradually a hierarchy of players began to emerge. Certain matches - mostly those involving Seward - took on the status of legend.

Seward once told me he used to dream about the Queen of Spades, a woman with coal-black hair and a steel bayonet. When I'm with her, he said, I can feel the point of her bayonet pricking my stomach. I can feel the sweat pouring off me, and I'm so frightened I keep thinking I'm going to wet myself, only at the same time I want it, I want her steel inside me. Do you think I'm mad?

I told him no, I didn't think he was mad. People with special gifts are sensitive, that's a well known fact, I said. My words seemed to comfort him at the time, but as conditions at the Front worsened, Seward became increasingly unbalanced, and increasingly mentally dependent on his luck at cards. It was as if the game represented his one remaining control over his life, and any small loss or setback upset him disproportionately as a result. He regressed into himself, his vitality only returning when he was actively participating in a round of cards. He talked about his game strategies all the time, so much so that some of the others believed he was bad luck and began to avoid his company.

During the final week of his life, Seward began to lose, culminating in one disastrous evening where he was landed with the Queen of Spades four games in a row. He was killed the following day, trapped in a dugout by four Germans and bayoneted. When we retrieved his body eight hours later we found that most of his midsection had been hacked into pulp.

A corporal from Hackney named Villiers inherited Seward's cards, and to some extent his luck, though the games became less intense after Seward was gone, there seemed less at stake.

A month after that, Villiers was dead too.

Nigel Seward's real name had been Nigel Fletcher. He was a milk-skinned, softly spoken lad, a physical weakling, the kind of man who got called a nancy even when he wasn't. As it happened, Fletcher was married, but if it hadn't been for his preternatural skill at cards, Beaumont had no doubt the rest of the unit would have given him a hard time. As it was, his luck at the game granted him an exemption, a notoriety that was even enhanced by his physical weakness.

Beaumont liked Fletcher, but it was clear to him from an early stage that he would not survive. Writing about Fletcher brought him back to life, at least for a while. Beaumont was used to writing essays, to explaining himself on paper, but the act of writing down anything this personal felt strange to him. He could not help noticing how inferior his observations seemed with Stephen Lovell's. In the war diaries Lovell had asked him to give to Rose Thorpe, every image seemed to be backed up by a cogent argument. Beaumont's writing was simply itself, a description of things that had happened and little more. Beaumont did not know if it was any good. He knew only that writing about Fletcher and his card games had made him feel he was doing something that made sense.

For a week he kept the typewritten sheets hidden in his desk, not certain what, if anything, he should do with them. Then he placed them in an envelope and sent them to *The Fiery Furnace*, a literary periodical he knew Dickie Ferguson had subscribed to. For the first hour after he posted the envelope, Beaumont was filled with a sense of quiet exaltation. After the hour had elapsed he became increasingly nervous, convinced he'd made a grave mistake, that what he had naively thought of as 'his writing' would reveal him as a charlatan and a fool. He entertained fantasies of rushing down to the postal sorting office and retrieving his envelope before it could be delivered, or of writing to *The Fiery Furnace*, insisting that his submission had been a mistake and should not be read. To alleviate his distress, he did his best to convince himself he was working himself into a frenzy over nothing, that the best thing to do was to forget about the envelope altogether. He told himself his submission would most likely remain, unopened, on somebody's desk until finally someone decided to throw it away.

A fortnight later Beaumont received a letter from the editor, saying that his essay was interesting and unusual and that they would like to publish it. Beaumont experienced a satisfaction that seemed out of all proportion with the level of his accomplishment. He supposed that this was because in writing about the war he had taken a step towards doing something that might eventually make sense of the life he had returned to.

Fletcher's death had been as pointless and as horrific as the thousands of others. But in naming his fate, Beaumont had at least granted Fletcher some of the dignity that was his due. Fletcher was a part of history now, and that could not be erased.

In a sense, Nigel Fletcher was still alive.

Outwardly, Beaumont kept his feelings closely guarded. He told no one about his debut as a published writer, fearing that his excitement would be judged as arrogance, and dismissed. It was Lovell he wished he could talk to, but Lovell was dead. When he saw an advertisement for a junior reporter's post on the *Clapham Gazette*, he applied at once.

"You won't get the meaty stuff, not for a while, anyway," the editor told him when he presented for his interview. "A fussy education won't do you any favours at the *Gazette*. We want people who can turn in copy and work to a deadline."

Beaumont reassured him he didn't mind what stories he was assigned, so long as he was given a chance to prove himself. "Even the most trivial story can sound exciting if you tell it properly," he said. Afterwards, thinking how green he must have seemed, he blushed at the memory.

The editor told Beaumont he could start the following week.

When he broke the news to Lucy she seemed pleased, but distant. The process of acquiring the lease on the Kennington Road premises was finally complete, and Lucy's whole world now seemed to revolve around the buying of stock, and the hiring of a suitable shop assistant.

"These girls," Lucy said. "They're just out of school, most of them. They don't seem reliable." It took Beaumont a second or two to realise she was still talking about the young women she was interviewing for the shop job.

"It should bring in some money, at least," Beaumont said, meaning his job at the *Gazette*, but Lucy was already half way out of the room. Beaumont remembered how little interested she had seemed when he had told her about Martingale. This was only natural, Beaumont reasoned. Lucy had never met the man, after all. But he knew that something final and irrevocable was happening, nonetheless, that they were drifting apart. Beaumont made no move to halt the process, even though the thought of losing Lucy made him feel sad and full of regret.

What Lucy herself was feeling he had no idea.

His second article for *The Fiery Furnace* took Beaumont longer to write, and seemed if anything less effective than the first. He redrafted it several times before submitting it.

Afterwards he wrote a letter to Rose Thorpe, asking her to meet him at a coffee house he knew close to Regent's Park. He sealed the letter in an envelope and stuck on a stamp, then tore the whole thing into pieces and threw it away.

Since finding success with *The Fiery Furnace*, Beaumont's visits to Billie's rooms had begun to take on an unsavoury aspect in his own mind, his sexual possession of her something he continued more from habit than from desire. It would not have been so bad, he reflected, if Billie were being paid for her compliance. As things stood, she seemed more and more to assume that Beaumont entertained genuine feelings for her when for Beaumont's part at least this was not the case.

He liked Billie, but there was no place for her in his life. None that made sense, anyway. He knew things had to change. He toyed with the idea of simply stopping his visits – Billie had no idea where he lived, so any likelihood that she might cause trouble for him was remote – but in the end he decided this would be too callous. He owed her an explanation, at least.

I'll tell her I'm going overseas, he thought. I'll say I didn't mention it before because I knew she'd be upset. The lie seemed both plausible and final enough to cut short all arguments. He would have sex with her one last time, if she insisted, then he would leave. He wondered about taking her a farewell gift, a gaudy little something she could add to the rest of her trash. He didn't much like the idea of leaving anything of himself behind in that room, not because he begrudged spending the money but because of the nagging fear that such a present might one day be the cause of her being able to find him again.

That's ridiculous, he thought. He purchased a china horse from one of the bric-a-brac stalls close to the Pimlico underground, a cheap thing, but quite pretty, exactly the kind of object Billie would like. In spite of the watertight nature of his plan, Beaumont felt anxious, his nerves prickling with the same sharp sense of his own danger that had sometimes overtaken him just before driving his ambulance out into no-man's-land. Beaumont hated the thought of a scene, but it was not just that.

Later, on his way home, he thought of Fletcher, the way he always seemed to know which cards you were holding, even before the first trick had been played. Not precognition exactly, but pre-sensation. The feeling of tension in the air just before a shell landed.

He was often to wonder how differently his life might have turned out if he had simply broken off relations with her without saying anything, as he had intended originally.

The first thing Beaumont noticed was that Billie was wearing a dress he had never seen before. Usually when he visited she wore a house coat, or a velour skirt, teamed with one of the garish, low-cut blouses she wore for serving behind the bar. The new dress, of a dark blue jersey fabric, complemented her hair and eyes and showed off the curve of her bosom without revealing too much of it. It was the kind of garment Lucy might wear.

She looks rather mysterious, Beaumont thought. Almost shy. He sensed she had some bombshell of her own to drop, and wondered nostalgically how he might now feel if she told him she was engaged to somebody else.

"You look nice," he said. He handed her the china horse, wrapped in a sheet of pink tissue paper. The paper had been hard to find, and had cost him almost as much as the ornament inside it.

"What's all this," Billie said. She was blushing, which was most unlike her, and Beaumont was suddenly overcome by the urge to spit his news out first, before Billie had the chance to get started. Whatever she was intending to tell him, it must not be allowed to affect the outcome of their meeting.

"I have to go away soon," Beaumont said. "I wanted to give you something." Something to remember me by, or something to thank you? He wasn't sure which sounded worse, so he said neither. Billie's fingers, which had been plucking eagerly at the translucent pink paper, were immediately still.

"Going away?" she said. "Where?" The coarseness of her delivery, the harshly interrogative demand for an answer, revealed the truth of her origins at a single stroke, and wasn't it odd, Beaumont thought, that she asked 'where' instead of 'when,' or 'for how long?' As if she guessed the extent of his treachery in advance.

"I'm returning to Paris," Beaumont said. "I have a friend there."

"A friend? Some woman, you mean."

"A woman? No, of course not. He's someone I met in the army. He's found me a job. On a newspaper."

Beaumont cursed himself inwardly for letting his lies run on, for seeding them so liberally with the truth. He knew he should stay quiet, but there was something about the way Billie was looking at him, an expression of heartbreak mingled with outrage, that made him feel bound to keep explaining himself. She gazed down at the little pink packet in her hand, and for a moment Beaumont felt sure she was about to throw it at him, but then she appeared to think better of it. She dumped it down on the sideboard. The wrapped horse fell over on its side with an audible clunk.

She'll finish you if you let her, Beaumont thought, so don't let her. The words came to him out of nowhere, like words overheard in a public bar, or on a station platform, and Beaumont knew they were Vladek's words, so clear inside his head it was as if Vladek were there beside him in the room. Beaumont remembered Billie's tale of the man in the patched coat who had given her the Dresden harlequin. Could it have been Vladek? It did not seem possible. He laughed nervously. Billie flushed a deep shade of red.

"I suppose you would think it's funny," she said. "Men are such beasts. Even when you think you've found one that isn't, he turns out to be more of a monster than the rest of you put together." She was beginning to cry, the fat tears splashing down onto her cheeks, so round and so gleaming, like perfect beads of moisture forced from an eye dropper. Beaumont watched as one fell to the floor, its outline flexing and stretching like an amoeba's, spitting reflected light like the paltry diamond chips in Lucy's ring.

"Billie, I'm sorry, I wasn't laughing at you, honestly." He laid a hand on her arm, but she tugged it away.

"Don't touch me," she said. "If you think you can get round me that way you've got another thing coming."

Beaumont drew back. If the whole thing ended with her yelling abuse and ordering him out of her rooms that was fine by him. He would have preferred an amicable conclusion to their affair – he had enjoyed Billie's company very much, at least in the beginning – but if this was the way she wanted it, Beaumont was perfectly content to let her cast him as the villain.

"I'll write to you, of course," he said, knowing he would do no such thing, forgetting at least temporarily that he was not going to Paris, in any case, that he would be less than two miles from her across the river.

"No you won't, because you won't be going nowhere," Billie said. "You can't go. I'm pregnant. That's what I've been trying to tell you."

She dropped her arms to her sides and glared at him. Her look had an exalted quality, and Beaumont was reminded briefly of Fletcher in those moments just after he'd landed you with the Queen of Spades.

"I don't believe you," Beaumont said. The words came out unbidden, because they were the words he had to say, even if he knew in his gut that he was lying to himself. The new dress, the quiet sense of something bubbling under – everything leading up to Billie's confession suggested she was telling the truth, that she had prepared her speech long before she knew that Beaumont intended to desert her.

All Beaumont could hope was that she hadn't yet revealed her secret to anyone else.

"You'd better believe it," Billie said. "Or shall we let that little posh piece of yours decide?" She took a step towards him, thrusting her face forward until their lips were almost touching. He could smell her scent, the Yardley's *eau de cologne* she always used after bathing, and for a second Beaumont was seized with the desire to lean in and kiss her. Then the sense of her words, which had seemed at first to be a kind of nonsense, struck him full on.

"What on Earth are you talking about?" he said, already knowing.

"That girl you're seeing. The one with the dinky waist and the frizzy hair. I know all about her."

Beaumont fell silent. He thought of Lucy's hair, the fine blonde curls that clustered about her forehead and against her neck. The idea that Billie had seen Lucy – had in the literal sense *laid eyes upon her* – seemed impossible to fit inside his universe. It jostled the outer wall of his mind, jabbing painfully against his consciousness as it tried, again and again, to force itself in. It did not occur to him that he had known already for some time that he and Lucy would never be married, that their love affair was now finished, as whatever had existed between him and Billie was now finished. That it did not matter what Lucy was told, or what she found out, because what she thought or felt or said was no longer a determining factor in his life.

Beaumont thought only of the ugliness of the thing, the sordidness of it, the horror and contempt he knew would erupt in Lucy's eyes.

"You silly little bitch," he said. "You wouldn't dare."

Beaumont found that he was laughing again, not because he found the situation funny, but because the words that had burst out of him were so much of a cliché, the kind of crude but essential stage dressing you might find inside the props cupboard of any provincial amateur dramatics company. Still laughing, he grabbed Billie by the shoulders and shoved her backwards into the wall.

"You bastard," Billie screamed. "Let me go."

Her words were as hackneyed as his, Beaumont reflected, but in the case of someone like Billie he supposed that was to be expected.

"Say you won't tell her," he said. "Promise me." His voice sounded odd to his ears, a muttering roar. She's right, Beaumont thought. I am a beast, after all. His stomach churned with rage.

"I won't, I won't tell her. I swear." Billie was crying, not the diamond-bright tears of before but a snivelling wetness that coated her chin and cheeks with a messy sheen. She looks vile, Beaumont thought, and he remembered her as he'd first seen her, stooping down to get into the cab, the dressing gown coat. He thrust her head back against the wall. There was a dull thud, and Billie screamed. Beaumont hoped the noise downstairs in the bar would mask the sound. By this time in the evening, he thought, it probably would. He still felt enraged, by the fact that he could not disprove her lies, by his conviction that she had, in some sense, planned this, that she had so wantonly transgressed the boundary in his life that he had laid down for her. She was a schemer and a liar, and he was a fool. He tightened his grip on her arms, feeling his fingers sinking deeper into the flesh, body heat pouring out of her like a noxious gas. She was breathing hard. Her breath had a meaty smell, the reek of acetone. Lovell's breath had smelled like that before he died.

Beaumont recognised it for what it was: the stench of fear.

"Please," Billie whimpered. "You're really hurting me."

Beaumont's palms were slippery with sweat. The ugliness of the situation tormented him more than the danger. He knew he had to let go of Billie, but he knew also that the moment he did so would spell the end of everything. He had been a fool to hit her, for sure. She would rush downstairs to the bar, screaming that there was a maniac in her room, that she was being attacked. People would come running. Beaumont would be apprehended, searched, questioned, possibly arrested. If Billie persisted with her stories about being pregnant the situation would rapidly become worse.

Inevitably, his name would be made public. He would lose his job on the Gazette – it would be like what happened with Dickie Ferguson. Even if he didn't, there was still Lucy. God knows how Billie knew about Lucy, but she did – Beaumont supposed she must have followed him home one night. Now Lucy was a card Billie could dump on him, any time, like Nigel Fletcher and his bloody Queen of Spades.

What a filthy mess he had made of things. Billie was the weak link, the source of all his troubles, in every direction. The only solution to the problem was for her not to exist.

He pulled her towards him a little way, then thrust her backwards against the wall as hard as he could. There was a vile cracking sound, and Billie went limp in his hands. Her mouth gaped open, and for a moment Beaumont thought she was about to scream again, but the only sound that came out was a kind of vacant gasping. It was as if she had forgotten how to breathe. She felt heavy in his arms. A single spot of red was visible at the corner of her mouth. As Beaumont watched it began trickling gently downwards towards her chin. Her head fell forward suddenly, her forehead almost smashing into his. In the place where her skull had collided with the wall, Beaumont could see an irregular red-brown smear staining the wallpaper.

He lowered her to the floor. Now that she was on the ground, she appeared smaller and curiously harmless. Her eyes were open but empty, dull as stones. Beaumont knelt beside her and laid a hand on her chest. He thought he detected a heartbeat, but his own pulse was pounding so loudly he could not be sure. I'll just leave her here, he thought. I'll pretend none of this ever happened. It's only her word against mine, after all. And if she says anything to Lucy, I'll just deny it.

Don't be a fool, said Vladek. You have to end it, here in this room.

Beaumont's guts ached, and he remembered how it had been, sometimes at the Front, when someone was so badly injured there was no hope for him, or nothing that could be called hope and still have the same meaning. These creatures were more like living meat than men, and yet it was monstrous, how long they sometimes took to die. You could not look at them without feeling terror – not for them, but for yourself, lest the same thing happen to you – and wanting to bury your head in the mud until it was over.

If you could take a length of metal piping and finish them off, so much the better. Ambrose Weston had used his gun and that was better still.

Billie groaned, a deep, wounded sound that seemed not to come from her at all but from somewhere beyond her, perhaps even from the realm she was now glimpsing in her agonised sleep. There was foam on her lips, bubbles of expelled saliva mingled with blood. She's going to be sick, Beaumont thought, and in the next moment she was, the pale stream of vomit bubbling from her mouth and spilling down to coat her chin and the front of her dress. Her head remained immobile, and Beaumont saw that unless she received help immediately she would be in danger of suffocating. Once again, he considered just leaving her, but he knew that if he walked out of that room without knowing for sure that Billie was dead, the uncertainty would make a mockery of his sanity. He reached the poker out of the fire bucket – a single blow to the temple would be enough – but the memory of the sound her head had made as it struck the wall made him realise the task was beyond him. He stood up, glanced rapidly around the room, then hurried across to the sofa and snatched up a cushion. The cushion was soft and flat, its cover an elaborate patchwork of pink and blue hexagons.

Billie had sewn the cover herself, he remembered her doing it. She had cut out all those tiny hexagons by hand.

Beaumont brought the cushion down over her face in a single swift movement. He felt better once that was done. The sight of her blank eyes, her mouth, choked with her own vomit – these things seemed less extreme once they were hidden. Keeping both hands on the cushion, he seated himself astride her and began pressing down. He remained where he was, pressing down, for five minutes by his watch, and then added another five just to be sure. Billie didn't move once, although Beaumont felt certain there had been a moment when he felt the life go out of her.

What remained at the end was a block of flesh and nothing more.

Beaumont got to his feet, then stepped away from her and looked down. The cushion still lay flat on her face, and Beaumont thought about leaving it there but in the end decided this might be unwise. He lifted it by one corner and shook it out. It regained its original shape almost at once, and Beaumont placed it, with the clean side upwards, back in its original position on the sofa.

Billie's eyes were still open, but in fact she looked marginally less dreadful than she had before. Beaumont supposed this was because her face was cleaner – his use of the cushion had inadvertently removed most of the blood and vomit from her chin and from around her mouth.

Her stillness terrified him. It was like Lovell's stillness, which Beaumont had felt himself bound to, only this time he was bound in another way. There were many words for death, many ways to try and make it seem less than it was. People called death a visitor, as if it were something that could be invited, or sent away. Beaumont knew that in the case of Stephen Lovell, death had been opportunistic, a black cat cut from the night, a predator that had seen its chance and brought Lovell down. In the case of Billie Drew, death had been in the room with them all along, a timorous, shadowy thing that might not have shown itself at all had Beaumont not enraged it.

The dust from its wings still clung to his fingers. Beaumont could feel death in the room still, but Billie herself was gone, Her things – the cheap china ornaments, the carnival glass – gawped at Beaumont in shocked confusion from the corners of the room.

A drunken shout from the bar downstairs tugged itself free from the general tumult, bounced upward through the window and floated away.

Beaumont could have left then, but his eyes fell suddenly upon the Dresden harlequin, smirking at him from its accustomed place upon the mantelpiece. The manikin's motley, he noticed, was made up of almost exactly the same pink and blue as the cushion Beaumont had used to suffocate Billie.

As if in proud acknowledgement of the fact, the little man was grinning.

Beaumont stepped across Billie's outstretched carcass and plucked the figurine down from the mantelpiece. The porcelain was smooth and cool to the touch. A devious little monster, Beaumont thought, but elegantly made. He remembered his words to Billie, that she should take care of the harlequin, that it could be worth something. Might the theft of such an item not provide the police with a motive for murder when they came – as they would surely come – to look for one?

A common thief, caught in the act? A robbery gone wrong? A man might do anything when desperate or surprised, and everyone knew The Commoner's Arms attracted a rough clientele. Hadn't he always told Billie she should be more careful of the company she kept?

After a moment's hesitation, Beaumont pulled a handkerchief from his pocket and wrapped it around the harlequin, then slipped it into the inside pocket of his coat. It fitted easily. He knocked a few of the cheaper ornaments from the mantelpiece as stage dressing, watching with satisfaction as they shattered on the hearth.

He left the pub by the back stairs. The noise from the bar was considerable, and so far as Beaumont was aware he was seen by no one. Outside on the pavement he realised he'd left his present behind, the china horse, still wrapped in its pink tissue paper. For a moment or two he felt panicked, almost persuading himself he would have to return to Billie's rooms to retrieve it. He scolded himself for getting into a state over nothing. The last person to handle the package had been Billie herself. The china horse was a cheap and commonplace object, exactly the kind of mass-produced item that would prove impossible to trace. There had been twelve identical horses on the stall where he had purchased it. They sold a hundred a week, probably.

In any case, going back would be madness. He carried on walking.

He kept expecting something to happen but nothing did. His normal route home from Billie's would take him through Pimlico, but on that evening Beaumont found the darkening emptiness of the backstreets disconcerting. The quiet seemed to magnify every noise, and every noise seemed to be the running footsteps of imagined pursuers. He cut through to Vauxhall Bridge Road, losing himself among the shift workers making their homeward journey towards Vauxhall and Balham. Their physical nearness – the stink of their work clothes, the harsh braying of their London vowels as they called out greetings or swore at one another – gave him the sense that he too might be one of them, a working man returning home from his labours. The traffic hummed, a steady progression of buses and taxi cabs. The street lamps were lit, but there was still a dim light in the west, the faintest glow of pink, the afterglow of what had been a glorious sunset.

It was not quite nine-thirty, a warm May evening. As he crossed Vauxhall Bridge into Lambeth, Beaumont finally allowed himself to veer away from the main roads and enter the maze of narrower side streets squashed in between the Lambeth Road and Kennington Lane. He found a pub on Jonathan Street, the Muse of Lambeth, and although the reek of beer and cigarettes, the stolid glow of the saloon bar fire, were an unwelcome reminder of the place he had just escaped from, he forced himself to go inside and approach the bar. The pub was a small concern, and much less rowdy than The Commoner's Arms. Three elderly grouches, clearly regulars, leaned on the bar and pored over the racing results. Two younger men, grey and depleted-looking, sat at a corner table playing dominoes. Fresh from demob, Beaumont thought. He was relieved to see a man behind the bar and not a woman, fat-fingered and round-bellied, with florid cheeks and a loudly chequered waistcoat. His hair was greased back so smoothly it looked painted on. For some reason he reminded Beaumont of the dormouse in *Alice in Wonderland*. Or was it Ratty in *Wind in the Willows*? He couldn't remember. Beaumont ordered a half of bitter and then asked for whisky instead. The rodent barman gave him a sour look, but complied.

You shouldn't have changed your mind, Beaumont thought. That was a mistake. He'll remember that, if anyone asks. People always remember people who've annoyed them.

"Glorious evening," Beaumont said, trying to smooth things over. He wondered if he should offer to buy the man a drink, then decided that would be going too far in the other direction.

"Certainly is, sir." The barman twitched his lips in a half-smile and placed Beaumont's drink on the bar. The whisky was tawny-gold, the colour of hay fire. Beaumont handed the man his money, the exact change. The barman jingled the coins in his palm for a moment then rang up the sale. Beaumont was gratified to see he was already turning away to serve another customer.

Beaumont took his whisky and went to sit down. The whisky shimmered in the glass, its acrid smokiness disseminating quickly in the warm air, and Beaumont found himself savouring the first sip in advance, the dogged little punch to the stomach, the heady aftermath of luminescent calm. He seated himself in a curtained alcove, behind the domino players and close to the fire but with a clear view of the street door. If anyone came into the bar he wanted to see them. He took a slug of the whisky, and was immediately enveloped by a sense of equilibrium and wellbeing that was, if anything, even more satisfying than it had been in anticipation.

He took off his coat, being careful not to damage the china harlequin in his inside pocket. He felt glad he hadn't left it behind in Billie's room. If he had, the pub landlord would most likely have thrown it out along with the rest of Billie's junk. He wondered what was happening in Billie's apartment at that exact moment and supposed nothing. There was a chance her body had already been discovered, that was true, but that chance was remote. In all the evenings he had spent with Billie, no one had ever knocked on the door or otherwise disturbed them. It was possible she might have agreed to meet someone else later in the evening, but once again Beaumont thought it unlikely. She would probably not be missed until she failed to report for work the following day.

In a way, Billie's murder was still in the future. Until the door to her rooms was actually opened, the contents of the space behind did not exist. At this moment in time, Beaumont was the only person who knew Billie was dead. He could carry on sipping his whisky as if nothing had happened.

Now that he came to think of it, even the word *murder* was not an accurate description of what had happened. If he had gone to the pub with the idea of killing Billie, that would have been different, but he had done no such thing.

Matters had got out of hand, that was all.

The correct, the more precise word surely, was *accident.*

He took another sip of the whisky and felt better. He thought about going back to the bar and ordering a second glass, but decided that might be unwise. His mind felt clear now – more whisky could only muddle his thinking. Also he had to think of how it might look to anyone watching. A second glass, so soon after the first, might mark him out, might transform him from a man enjoying a nightcap at the end of the day to a solitary drinker with something onerous on his mind.

He would be better to finish the whisky he had, and then leave.

Beaumont thought how strange it was, that he had endured a military tribunal and the contempt of his peers in order to assert his right not to kill his fellow human beings, yet he had ended up killing anyway, in circumstances as bizarre and as ugly as much of what he had witnessed at the Front.

If he had wanted to kill so badly, Beaumont reflected, he should have taken the precaution of committing his murder while under licence. He flicked the rim of his glass and smiled, appalled at himself yet amused nonetheless by the ironic turn his thoughts had taken. He remembered the way he had laughed just before he smashed Billie's head against the wall. What was it people said about the laughter of the insane?

The harlequin was laughing, too, he thought. He touched the china figure again through the cloth of his coat, He could almost believe it had changed position in there, curled on its side and fallen asleep, like a miniature cat.

So long as he kept it with him, Beaumont thought, his

luck would hold. He gulped down the last of his whisky and made for the door. One of the domino players glanced up as he passed. His face was empty of expression, and the way the light flattened his features made it seem to Beaumont as if he were staring into the face of someone in a photograph. He wondered if this was how things would be from now on, if the world at large would recede into flatness, like one of the painted dioramas that decorated the seafront arcades at Margate and Hastings, whilst what he had done in Billie's room took on ever stronger colours and greater clarity.

The act would forever define him, as the acts of all criminals defined them, no matter how blameless their lives before, how ambitious or worthy their plans for what came after.

Beaumont had thought the death of Stephen Lovell would be the memory that marked him, that bisected his life into two distinct halves, before-Lovell and after-Lovell.

It seemed he had been wrong.

He stepped outside. The darkness was now complete. He realised that he was hungry. Normally when he went to Billie's she would cook him supper. That hadn't happened this evening, for obvious reasons. Now that he had become aware of his need, the thought of eating began to trump all other thoughts. He remembered how before the war he and Doris would often sit up late, eating buttered toast and drinking Horlicks and setting the world to rights. Beaumont would read aloud to her from Machiavelli, and Doris would argue that despite the grandeur of his prose, Machiavelli was mistaken in his theorising, that the forces of entropy within the princedom would always finally prove stronger than the prince himself.

"It's in the nature of power," she would say. "Power exists in order to be overthrown."

Beaumont missed these conversations, he realised. But then he had barely spoken to Doris since his return from Paris. Not about anything that mattered, anyway. Was that her fault, or his?

He came to the house. He gazed up at its tall facade, yellowish in the lamplight. A light burned in one of the upstairs windows. He unlocked the front door, closed it softly behind him. The hallway was silent, but Beaumont thought he could sense a human presence, nonetheless. He imagined one of the lodgers kneeling on the floor in his room, rifling through the battered brown valise. The idea filled him with panic, even though he knew there was nothing to find.

Lucy was waiting for him on the second floor landing.

"It's late," she said. "I was worried."

"I've been walking around, that's all," Beaumont said. "Thinking what I might write about. You know, for the paper. Walking helps me to think." He drew her towards him and kissed her, his hands gripping the smooth rounds of her shoulders through her dressing gown. It was a pretty gown, in the style of a Japanese kimono, a sample of one of the lines she was thinking of stocking in the shop. She feels so warm, Beaumont thought, so alive. He thought of Billie, rapidly cooling now, her body and limbs stiff and meaningless, a mound of dead meat.

The difference between life and death was less than a second, he reflected, and yet it would be easier to cross from one side of this universe to the other than to bridge the infinite gulf between what Billie had been before and what she was now.

"You've been drinking," Lucy said. "I can smell it."

"Just the one." Beaumont smiled at her, wishing there was something of her beauty he could capture and keep, something of himself he might give to her in return, to let her know that for a while he had loved her, that his happiness had once been defined by her existence. "I stopped for a nightcap on the way home. It was such a nice evening."

He kissed her again. For a moment he considered asking her if she would stay the night in his room, and some part of his thoughts must have transmitted itself to her, because she did not move away from him at once, as she had begun to do recently, but pressed herself close, looking into his face, her mouth part the way open, as if ready to answer his unspoken question with a yes.

The thought that Lucy might one day know the truth of what he had done appalled him. He did not want their final moments together infected by the thought of it. He released her shoulders and took both her hands in his.

"Goodnight, Lucy." His heart turned over at the sound of her name. A thing of simple, untarnished beauty, it seemed already to have moved beyond his reach.

"Goodnight, Den," Lucy said. She lowered her eyes. Her cheeks were slightly flushed. "I hope you sleep well."

She turned away from him and started down the stairs. Beaumont never saw her again.

He slept for a couple of hours, then awoke and started packing his things. There was not much he wanted, books mainly, but even these he kept to a minimum. After some hesitation he decided he would wear his army greatcoat. The weather was too warm now for it to be comfortable, but it was a good coat, and would be expensive to replace.

He had planned to leave without a word, but changed his mind, scribbling a brief note to Doris, enough to let her know that he had left of his own accord. Hopefully that would be enough to stop her calling the police.

I am going away, he wrote. *I am not in any danger or trouble, but I need time to bring my life into order and so you might not hear from me for a while. Please tell Lucy that I am sorry, and that she is free. I hope you will both forgive me for any pain I have caused.*

He sealed the letter inside an envelope and placed it on his night stand. With any luck it would be some hours before they realised he was gone – plenty of time for him to get to Dover, and away. He thought it unlikely he would ever return. It came to him that this was what he had wanted all along, to abolish his old life completely and begin again, unburdened by a past that no longer fitted any future he would wish to inhabit. He had achieved that, at least. Such a severance was no longer a matter of choice, but of practical necessity.

He carried his knapsack and valise out onto the landing. The house, which should have been silent at this hour, seemed somehow alive, and after a moment Beaumont realised he could hear music. He descended to the first floor landing, then stood still and listened. In one of the lodgers' rooms, a gramophone was playing Debussy's *Clair de Lune*. The sound was turned down very low, but in the early morning stillness Beaumont was able to make out every note. It was a sad music, and it struck Beaumont as sad that someone else in the house should be awake at this hour, listening to Debussy's music on their own.

How little we know of one another, he thought. He wondered if whoever was behind the door was listening to him also, wondering where he was going and what he would do when he arrived there.

A brotherhood of the dead hours. For an instant it even seemed possible to Beaumont that the unknown listener might know his secret. Beaumont tightened his grip on his suitcase and carried on down the stairs. The ground floor hallway seemed to float up to meet him, a flickering tessellation of black and white squares.

The black squares yawned wide, like the mouths of tunnels.

He opened the door to the street. The dawn air rubbed itself against his cheek, soft and grey as the muzzle of an aging cat. At the edge of the pavement a fox, the fire of its pelt subdued by the morning mist, turned its yellow eyes briefly upon him then vanished into one of the gardens across the road.

Vladek, Beaumont thought. You old devil.

"Can I come in?" Beaumont said. Rose peered at him through the gap and then opened the door. Beaumont's memories of Rose Thorpe had become vague, blurred by the passage of time and by his own fear that he would forget her. Now that she was standing before him he understood that he remembered her exactly.

"What do you want?" she said. She stood aside, allowing him to enter the house. The expression on her face was guarded, but not surprised. It was almost as if she had been expecting him.

"I need to talk to you," Beaumont said. "What I told you before – that wasn't the truth. Not the whole of it, anyway. I want you to know the truth about how Stephen died."

"So now you're going to tell me some horror story," said

Rose. "I don't need those kinds of details, Mr Beaumont, I'm not stupid. I know that Stephen was in pain and probably frightened. Stephen was murdered. Murder is violent. Violence causes pain." She turned away from him, striding along the narrow hallway to her rooms at the back. Beaumont followed. It felt strange, and yet entirely natural to be with her, to be talking to her again at last, as if no time at all had passed since their previous meeting. "I loathe the war," she said. "Some days I loathe it so much I can barely speak."

"He was in pain," Beaumont said. "A lot. But he wasn't frightened. Stephen was a brave man. I didn't know him for long, but I do know that."

They were in her apartment. The place seemed brighter than before and less chilly. Beaumont supposed this was mainly because of the milder weather, but he noticed other small touches of warmth in their surroundings also: a bouquet of purple-tinged marguerites in a glass vase, a book – Katherine Mansfield's *In a German Pension* – laid face downwards on the kitchen table.

A green canvas suitcase, half-filled with things, lay open on the floor of the living room.

Beaumont looked at the suitcase and then looked back at Rose.

"I'm going away," Rose said. "I'm giving up the flat. There's no point in staying. Not now." She was trying to make it sound final, Beaumont thought, a decision that could not be changed and was therefore unworthy of discussion. But he sensed also that she was pleased he had come, that she had waited for him even. If I don't ask her where she's going, she will come with me instead, he thought. He tried to imagine himself sitting beside her on the train, their suitcases piled together on the luggage rack. It was surprisingly easy, and for a second Beaumont considered telling her everything. Billie's death, and his part in it. But it was all too close still.

"I'm going away, too," he said instead. "I have a present for you."

He dug into his pocket and took out the china harlequin, still wrapped in his handkerchief.

"What's this?" Rose said. She took the figurine from his hands, disentangling it from the handkerchief, which fell to the floor. She held the manikin upright. "Oh, he's very nice," she said. "What a lovely thing." She turned the harlequin to face the sunlight, stroking the pink and blue glaze. She looked genuinely delighted. Beaumont smiled. He would never have guessed that his gift would have such an effect on her, and he wondered what bright memory the little figure had reawakened.

Or perhaps, like Billie, Rose simply had a fondness for pretty things.

"I happened to see it in a shop window, and thought you might like it," Beaumont said. "I doubt it's worth anything."

"I don't care a jot about that." She was still gazing at the figure, clearly captivated. "Did you know that the character of the harlequin in mediaeval theatre was often supposed to be a stand-in for the devil?"

Beaumont laughed. "Don't tell me that's why you like him?"

Rose turned to look at him. "Would it bother you if I did?"

"Not in the slightest. It's just something I never heard before, that's all."

"That's because there was a Renaissance cover-up. The *commedia del arte* portrayed the harlequin as a glutton and a fool, an entertainment at the harlequin's own expense. But in the older mystery plays, Harlequin was Satan's servant, sent to Earth to round up sinners and bring them back to Hell." She held the figure level with her face and gazed into its black, pinprick eyes. "I've never gone along with that, myself. I've always seen the harlequin as a free spirit, the joker in the pack. He's capable of both good and evil – the point is that he's unpredictable. There was a story in the papers," she said, "about a harlequin leading some trapped soldiers out of the trenches."

"I heard it was an angel," Beaumont said. "A revenant from Agincourt, with a bow and arrow. War is full of stories like that. They're no better than fairy tales."

"All of them?"

"All of them." He could feel her waiting for him to drop his gaze, to laugh, to shrug free of the moment, but he would not do it. He thought if he could hold her and then die he would die happy.

"Tell me about Stephen," she said at last. "I want to know."

She sat down on the sofa, moving aside some clothes that were piled there. Beaumont did not know whether he should sit or remain standing but after a moment he sat down also, facing her. She seemed quite calm, different from the last time he had sat with her, here in these rooms, but then a lot of things had changed since then.

Stephen Lovell died in the back of an ambulance, in the yard of a burned-out farmhouse about a mile from the French market town of Cassaron. Stephen Lovell was a freelance journalist. He wrote feature articles about the effects of war on the civilian population. He travelled to India and North Africa, and lived for a while near Kardamyli, in the Peloponnese. He joined the British army as a volunteer. He wanted to experience the war from the point of view of a common soldier.

I knew none of these facts about Stephen Lovell until after he died.

Cassaron was destroyed because it was in the way. The town served as a German stronghold for a while, then the Allies staged a campaign to recapture it, not for any grand strategic reason but because there was a feeling that the Germans were getting too comfortable. It was a hard fight with many casualties on both sides, but in the end the Germans were driven back and Allied troops moved into the town and the surrounding countryside. Two days later, the Germans began to take the place apart. They made no attempt to recapture the town, just shelled it for forty-eight hours, reducing it to rubble in the process. It was what the sports pundits might refer to as a grudge match. The Allies saw the hopelessness of their position and withdrew, leaving the Germans to bomb the town into the ground.

What happened to the civilian population is not known.

When the bombing was over, Coulson and I drove out looking for casualties. The landscape was like no landscape I had ever seen before, blasted and desolate, like the terrible twilight future described in one of the novels of H. G. Wells. The bombing had been so severe that even the sky was mud-coloured, still choked with ash. The rain fell incessantly, turning the dust on top of the rubble to stinking grey putty.

There were very few bodies. We had been led to believe that the majority of the civilian population had fled before the main bombardment started. The few who had stayed would now lie buried beneath the rubble. I saw corpses here and there, soldiers mostly, cut down by mortar fire and so in a sense still running, forever in pursuit of a place of safety.

Most of these men were not whole. It was part of our duty to bring back the bodies and body parts for identification and burial, but after what happened to Coulson I ignored them. I had not slept for two nights because of the shelling, and following Coulson's death I became possessed by what I now suppose to have been a kind of madness. The ruins of Cassaron - no longer a town, no longer even the memory of a town - had made me begin to doubt the solidity of the world beyond. I kept thinking that Cassaron was just a taste of what was to come, the first tiny bruise on the skin of the apple that would eventually transform the whole to a stinking mulch.

If Cassaron - which just a week before had been a living, thriving organism, a network of streets and cafés and grocery stores and love affairs - could be reduced to a cinder, why not the rest of the world? All that was needed was a bigger bomb, and I felt suddenly and dreadfully convinced that it was only a matter of time before someone built one.

I wanted to bring someone out of that wasteland alive, if only to prove to myself that such a thing was possible.

I drove around, trying and mostly failing to make sense of the terrain. Now that no individual buildings existed, it was impossible to read the landscape as I had done before. Rather than houses and streets, I was forced instead to focus on the warped outlines of things that now lacked a clear context: the jutting stanchions of an incinerated road bridge, the toppled roundels of a torn-off chimney stack, the rubble-filled pit that had once been a mediaeval manor house. Such were my landmarks, and after a time and against my expectations I found myself learning how to interpret them. The wreckage of the town gradually reshaped itself in my imagination into something other, something greater than the sum of its dismembered parts, a cathedral of destruction possessed of a grandeur that was terrible and shocking but nonetheless real.

The town of Cassaron had been reconfigured as a temple to War.

Here and there I saw dark openings, the entrances to the coal holes and cellars of the houses that had once stood above them. I could not help but imagine how the mothers and grandfathers of Cassaron must have herded their children and their parents, their sainted aunts and invalid brothers down into the dark and cobwebbed cave system of bunkers and basements, hoping to wait out the bombardment underground. Now they were a town of troglodytes, their faces scarred by burns, their hands torn to shreds on fallen masonry as they battled to free themselves from their involuntary incarceration.

The people of Cassaron had not escaped, they had been buried alive. As darkness began to fall, my terror deepened. I was alone in the remains of a town populated by phantoms.

I drove in circles for more than an hour without seeing a single sign of life. The increasing darkness made the uncanny landscape all but impossible to navigate and the terrain was atrocious. On more than one occasion I found myself having to back the ambulance sharply and repeatedly just to get it going again. My arms ached from trying to control the vehicle on the torn-up ground. In the east, over towards the German lines at Goncourt, I could hear occasional gunfire and the thump of mortar rounds. It was time to head back.

The only reason I found Stephen Lovell is because I almost ran over him.

He was lying in a muddy hollow that might equally have been a shell crater or a roadside ditch. As the ambulance's headlights fell across his face he rolled over on his side, an arm curled about his head as if he were trying to protect himself from the onslaught of an aggressive predator. I jammed on the brakes immediately and jumped down.

"Are you hurt?" I called. "*Vous êtes blessés?*" I hurried to his side. It was disconcerting, I reflected, to find one man so absolutely by himself out here. If he was armed or dangerous in any way I would be seriously at risk. I had always refused to carry a gun myself.

He muttered something in reply but I was unable to make it out. I hunkered down, trying to see how badly he was injured. He was clutching at his stomach, curling himself around it as if trying to hide himself inside his own body. I took hold of his shoulder. The cloth of his flak jacket was soaked right through. I wondered how long he had been lying here.

"Can you stand?" I said. I could see nothing wrong with his legs, but by the light of the ambulance headlights his hands seemed to be covered with blood, and as I leaned in further towards him I began to smell the mixture of iron filings and filth that is the stench of a stomach wound. The flaps of his jacket were dark with his blood. I did not like to guess at the mess that lay beneath, though I had seen the same things before, or things like them.

The man's left cheek was slick with the mud on which he'd been lying. His eyes, twin grey stones, were bright with the alien light of his approaching death.

I ran to open the back of the ambulance, unrolling one of the khaki mattress pads that lay inside. It was clear that the man could not stand. In the absence of Coulson I was going to have to try and lift him myself. He was of average height only, and his slight build meant that under normal circumstances I might have been able to carry him the short distance without too much difficulty. But with the injury he had sustained, I knew the slightest movement was liable to be agony for him. The thought of having to get him up off the ground froze my insides.

I returned to his side. He raised his head at my approach, and I thought his movements seemed a little easier, perhaps because he knew he was no longer alone.

"I can drive you back in the ambulance, but I'm going to have to lift you. Do you think you can manage that?"

He nodded slowly. "Hurts like a bastard anyway," he said. His voice was faint and cracked, the voice of a distant moon-man speaking through a burst of radio static, but it established a connection between us. We were alone out there. We had to make the best of it.

"Hold on, then," I said. He knew what I meant at once, not that he should hold onto me, but that he should hold onto himself, that he should do what he could to steady himself against the pain. I bent down low, trying to muster the strength in my knees and ankles, bracing myself the best I could against the sodden ground. I slid one arm around his shoulders, the other beneath his pelvis, then hoisted him upwards, lifting him as I might have lifted a sleeping child.

He was a dead weight, made heavier by the mud and water soaking his clothing. He cringed in my arms and cried out. I lurched towards the van, almost slipping over in the writhing mud. He screamed again, and I felt the scream dive downwards into the straining muscles of my legs and arms.

It is he that is in pain, not you, I thought. He, not you. Not you. I let his cries grant me strength, let the vast hollow of his pain settle itself around the wholeness of my aching body. I felt it scrabbling, like a stick-thing, and then let go as I barked my shins against the metal steps that were folded beneath the open back doors of the ambulance. A dozen steps, no more, but we were here. I let the injured man drop down on the khaki bedroll. I felt the air race out of him, and for a moment I thought the shock had been too much, that he had died after all, but then I realised I could smell his breath, acrid as nettles. It fluttered, like a moth's wing, against my cheek.

He was still clutching his stomach. His eyes were closed.

"Shall I stop?" Beaumont said to Rose. "Is it too much?"

Rose shook her head. Beaumont saw that there were tears on her cheeks, and that her eyes were closed also, shrouded against the pain as Lovell's had been. He knew that whatever she was seeing inside her head would not be as bad as what Lovell had suffered, that Lovell's pain could not be assimilated by mere imagination. Lovell had been brave, though – Beaumont had not lied about that. After those moments of near-unconsciousness, he had thanked Beaumont for helping him, and when Beaumont offered him water he had taken a sip, even though he no longer possessed a stomach fit to receive it.

"How long did he live, after?" Rose asked.

"A couple of hours," Beaumont said. "I laid a blanket over him, and closed the back doors. Then I climbed into the front seat and began to drive. It was completely dark by then and I wasn't sure how far we were from the field hospital but I guessed we'd make it back in about half an hour. I don't know what happened," he said. "I must have lost my way somehow, doubled back. It seemed like I was driving forever. Then the ambulance got stuck in a pothole. I jumped down, rocked it back and forth a bit the way you're supposed to. It wouldn't budge. It needed two people to shift it."

"You shouldn't have been out there alone," Rose said.

Beaumont nodded. He thought of Coulson, drowning in flame. "I had to give up in the end. The van was stuck and I was exhausted. I had no idea where we were. I knew I had to wait until it got light – at least then I could walk out, find help that way. But Stephen died before that could happen."

He told Rose how he had climbed into the back of the van with Stephen, how Stephen had remained conscious for a little while and had even taken a little more water. "He talked about you," Beaumont said. "He told me your address, said I should come and find you when I got home. I said I would if I could. He seemed happier after that, more peaceful. He died soon afterwards. I stayed beside him until the morning. I even slept for a while. Once it was light I discovered that the ambulance was standing in what had once been a farmyard. There was a burned-out house, a pigsty. We were much closer to the main road than I had realised. I started to walk in what I hoped was the direction of the field hospital. After about an hour a friendly convoy turned up. They took me with them."

It was a version of the truth, a partial image that Beaumont hoped Rose would be able to accept. The parts about Lovell and herself, at least, were true in their entirety. "Are you all right?" he said at last. "I'm sorry if it's painful, but I thought you should know. I wanted you to know everything."

"I'm all right." She inhaled deeply, shudderingly, as if she had been swimming underwater and had just broken the surface. "I feel better than I have done since I first heard Stephen was dead. It's as if he were here again, really with me. I know I'll never see him again but now –." She broke off suddenly, wiping at her eyes with the back of her hand. "Now it's as if that doesn't matter because he'll always be with me."

"I'm glad I could help," Beaumont said.

"I want to thank you for helping Stephen. And for coming here and telling me about his death. That took courage, I know. You're a good man."

She touched his hand briefly. He felt the warm tips of her fingers, brushing his skin like the unfurling shoots of tender spring leaves. Beaumont knew that she was touching him not out of care for himself but for Lovell, because of her love for another man, and her feeling that through an accidental miracle some portion of their togetherness had been restored. For an instant he felt a jealousy of Stephen Lovell so profound it was like hatred, a raging blackness inside that made him almost glad that Lovell had died in the way he had.

He thought this bitter aftertaste of death must be his real punishment for killing Billie.

Then he remembered that he was alive and Lovell was dead. Whatever fantasies Rose chose to entertain, her time with Lovell was over. For Beaumont, the game was still in progress. His hand was not yet played out.

"You said you were going away," he said. "Do you mind my asking where?"

"I'm going abroad. To Argentina. An uncle of mine has a *hacienda*, a large acreage to the north of Buenos Aires. He wants to set up a school there, for the children of the men who work on the ranch. I've said I'll go and run it for him, at least for a time." She paused. "I can't imagine what my life will be like, and that's at least partly why I want to go. It's so easy to believe that the life you were born into is the only life you can lead, that the rules of the world you know are the real rules, that everything outside that circle is somehow inferior, unreal, even. I find that to be the worst kind of arrogance, the death of the mind. I want to find out who I really am, what I'm capable of. It's an adventure, and I need an adventure. I know Stephen would want me to go."

Beaumont experienced despair, so sudden and so total it was as if he had been remade, as if the person he had been until then could not survive the disappointment. He had found her, and now she was going. He drew in his breath, as if he had been burned.

"I thought we might see each other," he said. He had told himself that in coming to her, he was trying to balance what he had done to Billie with one right thing, to pay off evil with good. He saw now how pathetically he had deceived himself, not just in believing he could somehow atone for Billie's murder but in lying to himself about his true motives. He had intended to ask Rose to go away with him to Paris, to make some kind of life together. He had not dared to think about how their togetherness might manifest itself. Just so long as he could keep her in his life.

Beaumont had believed ever since Cassaron that the war had made him mad, that his perception of reality had become skewed in some way. It was almost comforting to discover that he was also susceptible to madness in its most commonplace and contemptible form: he was still capable of deluding himself over a woman.

"I'm not good company at the moment," Rose said. She smiled. "But we could write to each other, if that doesn't sound too dull. Letters can be a lifeline, don't you think?"

"I do," Beaumont said. He thought of Lucy's letters, which he had burned in the stove, in his room in Pigalle before he left Paris for England, and then tried to imagine receiving a letter from Rose, its pages touched by the southern hemisphere, the atoms of her breath caught in the folds of paper and then despatched to him. "I would be honoured to write to you."

She laughed.

"If you let me have your uncle's address, I'll write and let you know mine as soon as I'm settled."

"You're going away also?"

"I'm returning to Paris," Beaumont said.

"To Paris? Are you planning to be away for long?"

"I don't know yet. Probably. London hasn't been the same for me since the war." He longed to tell her about his ambition to become a journalist, about the essay he had written for *The Fiery Furnace* about Nigel Fletcher and his obsession with the Queen of Spades, but he felt embarrassed suddenly, afraid Rose might think he was copying Stephen, that in some sinister way he wanted to *be* Stephen. Perhaps that was true even, or had been. But it no longer felt like the largest part of the truth.

It felt like the past. In talking with Rose, Beaumont had

freed himself of Lovell. What he did after today would be on his own account.

"Well, have a safe journey," Rose said. "Make sure you write to me." She stood up from the couch and went to a hardwood *escritoire* that stood beneath the window. She tore a leaf from an exercise book and wrote something down on it, her uncle's address, Beaumont presumed, in South America. He thought about the symmetry this new leave-taking seemed to form with their first parting, when he had written down the address of the Kennington house for her on the back of an envelope.

How could the world move on so far in so short a time?

He took the paper from her hand, and thought about what might happen if he tried to kiss her. He thought about her features softening as her eyes closed, her narrow chest, pressed against the closely woven grey worsted of his too-warm overcoat.

These things might happen, but the risk that they might not was too great to bear. All he needed to know of Rose was that she was alive somewhere, that he might one day see her again.

She walked with him to the station. It was another warm day, the bright air suffused with the scent of cherry blossom and spring greenery. Beaumont stepped onto the train, then pulled down the carriage window and waved. Rose raised her hand and waved back. It felt like the last moment of the known world.

On arrival in Dover, Beaumont bought his passage on a ferry that was due to sail for Calais at four o'clock, together with a train ticket for his onward journey to Paris. He took lunch at a restaurant on the quayside where the decor was shabby but where the food was surprisingly good. He finished off the meal with a cup of strong coffee. A couple who had been dining at the neighbouring table left behind a copy of the *London News*. When he felt sure they weren't coming back, Beaumont leaned across and scooped it up. He glanced quickly through its pages, then turned back again to the beginning and went through them more slowly.

There was no mention of a murder in a public house close to Victoria station. Either Billie's body had not been discovered yet, or it had been discovered too late to make the morning papers.

By the time the evening editions hit the newsstands, Beaumont would be halfway to Paris. He wondered how much time would have to elapse without news – days, months or years – before he could bring himself to believe there was a chance the murder had never happened at all.

He thought of Billie's china harlequin, grinning and grinning.

The ambulance is stuck fast. My boots and combats are splattered with mud. I lean against the side of the van, the metal pleasantly cold against my cheek. I know that Lovell is done for unless I can get him to a hospital. Most likely he is done for whatever. I think of the bloody, tattered flaps of his combat jacket, the stinking, rancid darkness beneath. How much of a man has to be destroyed before he stops being a man?

It is a relief simply to stand still and do nothing. After a while I realise I am thinking about Coulson again, the awful thing that happened to him with the incendiary. The way he twisted as he fell, outlined in flame, still screaming.

I did not run to help him. Not only because it was hopeless, but because I was afraid that I would die alongside him and in a similar way.

I get back inside the ambulance and start the engine. It's useless, but I don't know what else I can do. I take my foot off the accelerator and lean my head against the steering wheel. If Lovell were already dead it would be easier. I could begin my walk out of here, back towards the road, towards shelter, towards nothing at all perhaps but away from here. But Lovell is not dead, and I know I will not leave him as I left Coulson, not because I am a better man now than I was two hours ago, but because it is dark and I find Lovell's presence reassuring, even though I know he is going to die.

I hear the tapping in my mind before my senses acknowledge that it is real. A clear, pointed sound, at odds with the claggy, ash-soaked wind and the rainfall, so unrelenting I have ceased to notice it.

There is someone outside the ambulance, knocking on the window. For half a second I am convinced it is Coulson. He has followed me after all, determined to be rescued, his cooked flesh caked to his bones like strips of braised pork. Beyond the pale, no longer human, my enemy. I shrink inside my skin, feeling nothing but the terrified desire to get away.

The tapping comes again, the insistent,

repeated battering of carbon on silica. I turn, because in the end I find it impossible to keep hearing that sound and not respond to it.

The figure I see at the window is not Coulson, but my heart leaps up nonetheless, because still there is a man where none should be. Not in that wilderness, at least none living. He is stooped over, peering in at me through the glass. His face in the light from the headlamps is pale and long, the jutting, aquiline nose its most prominent feature. His hair, plastered to his skull in the drenching rain, tangles messily about his shoulders. The coat he wears is long and belted, also soaked with rain. I see him mouthing something, words I should be able to hear but cannot quite make out. He gestures with his hand, tugging sharply downwards on an imaginary handle. He seems irritated, but not hostile. Perhaps he wants a lift. That would make sense, I think, in this weather. At least it would make sense if the ambulance were not stuck in the mud. But then again, I realise, there are two of us now, we can move it.

I open the door.

"Hurry up," the man says. "Or this man will die."

He can only mean Lovell, although there is no way he can know of Lovell's existence. I toy with the idea that it is himself he is talking about, that he has a habit of talking about himself in the third person. He has a foreign accent, very slight. Is he a German? If he is, he does not seem to be carrying a gun, so I don't care much either way.

"The van's stuck," I say. "There's a pothole or something. Do you think you could help me try and shift it?"

"There's a rut on this side, you can see it, and a block of concrete impeding the wheel. If you start the engine I'll try to free it."

He sets his shoulder to the side of the van. I feel the vehicle shift, just a fraction, and I start the engine immediately. I can feel the change at once, the return of traction, the earthed power of a motor applying friction instead of the mindless spinning of weights about an untethered axis. I open the cab door, thinking it might be better if I jumped down and began pushing also, but my rescuer thinks differently.

"Keep up the pressure," he shouts. "We're almost there."

As it turns out, he is right. The engine groans, then gasps with surprise, then the van shoots forward. The sudden movement after the long period of inertia sends a shocking jolt through my shoulders and into my hands. I take my foot off the pedal and the van stops moving but it is now on level ground and free of the mud.

I turn back towards the passenger door, meaning to thank my mysterious helper and offer him a lift to wherever he might be headed but he is no longer there. A moment later his face appears in the open window on the driver's side.

"You are very tired," he says. "Let me

drive, and you can rest. The main road isn't far. I can find the way."

His suggestion is madness - to relinquish the wheel to a stranger, a stranger who might even be an enemy - but I realise it is the only suggestion I want to hear. My one desire is to sleep, to forget, and my rescuer is offering to take responsibility for what happens next.

If he drives me back towards the German lines I will be taken prisoner. Could such a fate be worse than being lost in no-man's-land, than being forced to witness what happened to Coulson? I reason not.

If I come to be questioned, later, about how I came to lose control of the ambulance, I will say that the man had a gun, that he took me hostage, that I had no choice.

I step down and walk around to the passenger side, holding onto the van to keep my footing in the slippery ground. By the time I have lifted myself into the passenger seat the stranger is already behind the wheel.

"Are you an officer?" I ask him. The inside of my head roars with exhaustion. I wonder how I am still conscious.

"I have never been a military man," the stranger says. "The life doesn't suit me. As to sides, I am a neutral. You may call me Vladek."

"Is that Polish?" Now that I can see him more clearly, I realise there is indeed something Slavic in his appearance: the high cheekbones, the deeply set eyes.

"An interesting people, the Poles. Tenacious as terriers, honour over sanity, every time. I like them." He revs the engine and the van lurches forward. I close my eyes, surrendering myself to the motion, swooning into it as if it were rising water.

At some point I remember Lovell in the back of the ambulance. I wonder if he is still alive.

We drive. It could be for five minutes, or five hours. The world seems unreal to me, a paper world constructed for children to play with, and I keep sliding off the edge of it into sleep. Sleep, like a pit of black water. I am aware of the man beside me at the wheel. I am glad that he is there, that I am not alone. Finally we come to a standstill. There is a moment of stillness in which the only sound I can hear is the steady, muted rattle of rain falling on the roof of the ambulance. I can smell the cracked leather of the seats, the foam and horsehair stuffing beneath. It seems like I have been smelling it for years.

"We will be safe here for a while," Vladek says. "We are close to the road, but hidden. No one will see us. Now I want to have a look at your friend. Do you have a light?"

I am about to say that Lovell is not my friend, that I don't even know his name, but in the end I say nothing except to confirm that we have a storm lantern. We get down from the van and go around to the back. I still feel tired but I no longer feel crippled by tiredness, as I did before. I slide open the doors and hold up the lantern. Lovell is lying on his side on the khaki bedroll. The bedroll is soaked with blood. From the way he is lying and from his stillness I can see at once and without any doubt that Lovell is dead. I feel something well up inside me, a kind of hopelessness, together with a sense of guilt that he died alone, in the van, in the darkness, that for a good part of our journey I had forgotten about him entirely.

I stand still, holding the storm lantern. Vladek scrambles up inside the van. He is stocky but nimble, and for some reason I find myself thinking of an image in an old picture book of Doris's, Master Daddy Longlegs, a spindly creature in striped pyjamas who is sometimes a human being and sometimes a spider.

"He's a mess," Vladek says. "We need to get him cleaned up at once."

I watch, stupid and dumb, as Vladek raises Lovell in his arms and begins removing the slippery tangle of cloth that was once his flak jacket. There is a slapping sound on the floor of the van as he casts it down, and I know that no man can survive that much blood loss, that for Lovell to have any hope of coming through this he would have needed immediate attention in a field hospital. Even then he would probably have died later, from infection.

"He's gone," I say. My voice sounds too loud in the darkness.

"Not yet," Vladek says. "Hold the light steady, would you?"

He removes Lovell's service vest. At the centre where he was hit, Lovell's body seems pulverised, the flesh in clots, the glistening blackish red of smashed fruits. There is a smell like wet metal. The rest of his torso is smeared with a grainy mixture of mud and blood.

I look away, I cannot help it. The light shakes in my hand.

"Keep it still, please." Vladek lays Lovell gently back down on the bedroll, then wrenches open one of the overhead lockers. There are fresh dressings inside, and in another cupboard a length of cotton sheeting. Vladek forms a pad with the dressings, which he places carefully over the centre of Lovell's body. Then he wraps the sheeting snugly around him, like swaddling, like a winding sheet, and pins the whole thing tightly in place with four large safety pins.

Already, Lovell looks cleaner. He looks like a human being. But he is still dead. I don't know why Vladek has bothered, why he has chosen to waste perfectly good medical supplies making cosmetic improvements to a corpse. I begin to fear that Vladek is as mad as I am, some insane disciple of Friedrich Nietzsche who believes he can bring the dead back to life through sheer effort of will. Am I alone in the dark with a maniac? Then Lovell turns his head to one side on the blanket and vomits.

The vomit steams and stinks like pitch.

Lovell gasps and turns his head the other way. I see Vladek reaching for what remains of Lovell's service vest and using it to mop up the vomit. He throws the soiled rag out of the van.

"Try and lie still," he says to Lovell. I feel numb. I think perhaps that I am also dead, that what I am seeing is a kind of after-image, what the spiritualist cranks refer to as an out-of-body experience, the equivalent of the black and white motes that dance across the backs of your retinas after a camera flash has gone off. Vladek replaces the blanket over Lovell.

"This is just temporary," he says to me. "We still must get him to a hospital. He needs to see a doctor as soon as possible."

I set down the lamp on the floor of the van.

"I don't understand what just happened," I say. "That man was dead."

"He was very weak, that's all. He has lost a lot of blood." He wipes his hands on his coat, and I see a curious thing, that the coat is not all of a piece as I had imagined, but fashioned from irregularly sized patches of different cloth. Most of the patches are grey or French navy or khaki, dulled by the darkness to a homogenous sludge, but here and there I can see patches of brightness: squares of yellow and red, a spike of fox orange.

"What is that you're wearing?" I say. "Who the devil are you?" I grunt with impossible laughter. I feel tears welling up beneath my eyelids, scuttling for egress, hot and busy as the tiny black mice that constantly assail us in the trenches, searching for food.

"You are exhausted," Vladek says. He places a hand upon my shoulder. It has been a long time since anyone has touched me, apart from dead men. I shudder. "Listen, you did well. You have done as much to save this man as I have."

He produces a flask from his inside pocket. He unscrews the lid, then presses the mouth of the silver bottle against my lips. I taste brandy, whose acrid fumes remind me of the fire that devoured Coulson. I think of soup, hot coffee, and somehow the brandy seems to taste of all these things.

"He will sleep now," Vladek says, nodding at Lovell. "You should sleep, too."

He extinguishes the lamp and closes the ambulance doors. "I'll drive," he says. "Come."

I stumble around the side of the van and climb back into the passenger seat. A second later Vladek is beside me at the wheel.

"This war of yours," he says. "Tell me what you think about it. It intrigues me." He twists the ignition key. The engine starts first time.

"I think it's a form of mass hypnosis, visited on the people by the state," I say. I can only imagine that he is trying to make fun of me. What motive he finds in doing this I cannot tell. "And it's not my war. I refused to fight in it. I drive an ambulance."

"And you don't think that driving an ambulance is in itself an act of acquiescence to that hypnosis?" He backs the van a couple of feet and then drives forwards. There is a slight jolt, and then we begin to move more freely, almost as if the ambulance were travelling along an ordinary suburban street on the outskirts of London.

Vladek's hands grip the wheel. He does not look at me, but faces forwards, staring through the windscreen at the darkness beyond. From where I am sitting it is impossible to read his expression.

"I don't understand what you mean," I say.

"I mean that war is not just fighting and killing, it is also the industry that surrounds it, that keeps it going, that allows it to exist. Those who take money for making guns, for designing aircraft. Those who sing in music halls where soldiers find their entertainment, those who fuck the officers, who accept their gifts of clothes and perfume and money. Those who drive ambulances or treat the wounded or who make reports about the war in the daily newspapers. They are all part of the industry of war, and no war could continue without them. Or not for long." He pauses. "War is itself a commodity. People either purchase it, or invest in it, or use it as advertising. I believe that in the future, whole wars will be won or lost on the strength of advertising.

Bigger bombs, faster aircraft, more highly trained soldiers. I can see generals, browsing through catalogues of mass destruction in their underground bunkers, heads of state sipping fine malt whisky as they stake the lives of their citizens on a hand of cards."

"The Queen of Spades," I murmur. I am wondering if his words are really his, or just the sound of my own thoughts, somehow externalised. Perhaps Vladek is not here at all. Perhaps I am asleep at the wheel, about to drive the ambulance off the road. At least it is going slowly. Nothing will happen. It will simply stop.

"War exists," Vladek continues, "not as a noble pursuit or a means to an end but as an entertainment. Without war, men grow bored. War is invented anew for each generation. From the wooden club to the atom bomb, the eternal circle of denials and deceits."

What is an 'atom bomb'? My whole body aches. I think of Lucy, so many miles distant, and wonder if I will ever speak to her again. There is blood on my hands, more even than I know about. I know that Stephen Lovell cannot be alive.

We are driving through the darkness. Very soon I fall asleep, thinking how good it feels simply to be driven, to have no control or care over where I am going. I remember being driven in a hackney carriage back from a birthday party at a large house in Richmond. I am eight years old and overtired, tearful and fretful with excitement. A rug is laid over my knees. I fall asleep to the thud of the horses' hoofs.

When at last I wake, the first thing I notice is that it is no longer raining. The ambulance is parked on cobblestones, at the centre of what must once have been a stable yard. There is a burned-out house, a pigsty. There is no one around.

The seat beside me is empty. I get out of the van. My knees feel numb and weak, but that is mostly because I have slept sitting up. Once I am on my feet the feeling in my legs rapidly returns to normal. I walk as far as the house, which is a ruin, and then the barn, which is now no more than four iron uprights set into concrete foundations. I stand still, listening for voices, for footsteps, but there is nothing to hear.

I return to the ambulance. The rear doors are open. On the floor inside I see the soiled bedroll, the remains of a swathe of cotton sheeting, a bloodstained knapsack that turns out to contain papers and an ID tag belonging to a Captain Stephen Lovell. There is a photograph of a woman, a dirt-smeared envelope containing an unfinished letter. The letter begins: 'Dearest Rose'. The address on the envelope is for somewhere in Croydon.

Lovell is gone. I see footprints in the mud, so many of them, all overlapping. They could have been made days ago, before Cassaron was destroyed. They could have been made just minutes before I woke up.

I slam the rear doors closed, climb back into the driver's seat, key the ignition and begin to drive. In less than five minutes I come to the main road. I head east, making towards the supply unit and the field hospital. A short while later I catch sight of a British convoy, heading westwards towards what remains of Cassaron. The lead vehicle signals for me to pull over, and when the CO asks me the number of my unit, I give it at once.

"I must have lost them in the dark somehow," I say. "I've been out here all night. Any idea where they've got to?"

The CO shakes his head. "That unit's gone, I'm afraid," he says. "You'd better tag along with us for the time being." He looks me up and down, then glances past me towards the ambulance. "Motor's still in one piece, I see," he says. "Good show."

We continued westwards. I watched for signs of Vladek and Stephen Lovell on the road, but of course there were none.